ALIENS STINK!

ALIENS STINK!

STEVE COLE

ILLUSTRATED BY JIM FIELD

SIMON AND SCHUSTER

For Tobey & Amy
"Hello! Little G"

Thanks to Helen Giles for some astrophysical advice I took pains to garble

Images dedicated to Random Dad aka 'Papa-Razzi' Jim Field

First published in Great Britain in 2014 by Simon and Schuster UK Ltd • A CBS COMPANY Text copyright © Steve Cole 2014 Illustrations copyright © Jim Field 2014 • Design by Paul Coomey • This book is copyright under the Berne Convention No reproduction without permission • All rights reserved • The right of Steve Cole and Jim Field to be identified as the author and illustrator of this work respectively has been asserted by them in accordance with sections 77 and 78 of the Copyright, Designs and Patents Act. 1988 • Simon & Schuster UK Ltd • 1st Floor, 222 Gray's Inn Road, London WC1X 8HB • www.simonandschuster.co.uk • This book is a work of fiction. Names, characters, places and incidents are either the product of the author's imagination or are used fictitiously. Any resemblance to actual people living or dead, events or locales is entirely coincidental • A CIP catalogue record for this book is available from the British Library • PB ISBN: 978-0-85707-872-8 • eBook ISBN: 978-0-85707-873-5 • Printed and bound by CPI Group (UK) Ltd, Croydon, CR0 4YY • Simon & Schuster Australia, Sydney • Simon & Schuster India, New Delhi • 10 9 8 7 6 5 4 3 2 1

ZERO

I sat frozen on the bed. Staring.

Three dark eyes stared back

and winked at me in sequence.

There was a living creature in my holdall.

It was like nothing on Earth.

It was **ALIEN.**

ALIEN, I TELL YOU!

But to be honest, I'm getting ahead of myself. We

shouldn't really meet the **ALIEN** until page **78**.

DON'T FLICK THERE NOW TO SEE!

(Or if you must, be quick, OK?)

I need to tell you

how the whole thing came to happen.

And **YOU**

need to turn the page.

PART ONE

MY DAD,
FIST-FACE
and the early stages
of the cosmic crisis
soon to endanger
our world

(and me)

ONE

Let me paint you a little picture of my dad and me.

Or, draw you one, anyway.

TIM GOOSEHEART
FREAKO-WORRIER

"How hard can it be?" you're thinking. "So your dad cycles around the place, hugs a few trees, goes on protest marches . . ."

YOU'RE THINKING WRONG.

I can see I need to give you examples.

Take our house for instance.

I always wished someone would. The binmen, if possible.

Because our house is RUBBISH.

6

Actually, it really *is* made out of rubbish, wrapped up in some weird eco-concrete stuff. Dad designed the place himself, so it makes its own electricity and even recycles our water. It took him years to build it on some wasteland he bought cheap, next to an old windmill. He started when I was nine years old, and finally finished building it when I was twelve. During that time, we rented a normal house like normal people.

Those were good years.

New Scientist magazine called Dad's dream-come-true, "The world's ultimate green home".

The local paper called it, **"FLOWER-POWER EYESORE HATED BY BAFFLED NEIGHBOURS"**.

And Darren "Fist-Face" Gilbert in the year above called it, "The stinking, mouldy freak-dump where gimpy Gooseheart sits on his own crying all night cos everyone hates him, then uses the tears to wash his bum because he's too poor to use normal water." Which, you know, wasn't so good.

And not even true. I've definitely never EVER washed my bum with tears. Tears are salty for a start. Who wants a salty bum?

I know why Fist-Face said stuff like that though. Kids always pick on anyone who's different, don't they? I've tried telling this to Dad, tried telling him I want to be normal. But he's been daring to be different his whole life and wants me to be that way too. "Don't be afraid to stand out, Tim!"

Easy for Dad to say – well, unless he's saying it through a mouthful of organic tomatoes, which he probably is. Because, worst of all, Dad grows organic veg in our garden and that is **ALL WE EAT!** Mmmmm.

I could go on – about Dad's jumble sale shopping sprees, about Dad's protest marches outside fast-food stores (where me and him are the only two who've shown up, and me only because he'll ground me if I don't), about how we can't have a car because that would make us evil polluters and so on and so on and so, **SO** on.

But you see how it is. Dad might be trying to save the planet, but **NOBODY** can save my rep!

I hope you can understand how, some nights, I

would lie awake thinking,

"PLEASE, WON'T SOMEONE MAKE THIS TORTURE END?"

So maybe it's all my fault. Because, as it turned out, fact fans . . . Yes. Someone *would* make this torture end. But not in a good way.

TWO

Dad works at the Space Centre. The Space Centre is not, in fact, the centre of space, but a place in the city where clever people do research into Crazy Out-There Physics stuff, and Amazing Things To Do With The Structure Of Space And The Universe.

Don't ask me what Amazing Things Dad did there – it was all a big secret.

Was he . . .

☐ Doing weird experiments on alien brains?

☐ Sending unwitting test subjects into space?

☐ Bunking off to Mars with his mates?

I wish I did know what Dad was getting up to. I was born around the time he started there, and every time I've asked, he's never once told me.

"You wouldn't understand, Tim," he says. "And if you *did* understand, I'd have to fire you into the centre of a black hole because it's super top secret and no one is allowed to know." And then he normally does his crazy-sounding laugh.

I still want to know, but other than Dad, there's not really been anyone else to ask.

"What about your mum?" you say.

Well, I don't have a mum. Thanks for bringing that up! No, really – **THANKS**. I appreciate it.

Nah, it's **OK**. Don't feel bad. Much.

I'm over the whole thing, really. I've had to be. Dad won't talk about it.

He looks shifty and says I was brought to this world by aliens and left on his doorstep.

I **THINK** he's joking, but who knows? Certainly not the other forms of life who've shared my home –

like Nanny Helen (that's "nanny" as in "childminder", not as in "grandma" or "goat") and Herbert, my pet goldfish. Neither of them knows a thing. (Or if Herbert does, he's playing it cool.)

It makes me think sometimes, when things feel hard here and I look up at the night sky . . . could it be that I belong out there?

Life has got to be easier out there in space.

Right?

THREE

So when does this story really start? Well, right now, with the Beginning.

And the Beginning began with the Big Heal.

You remember? That's what they called it – the Big Heal. Also known as the Green Miracle, or the Night the World Got Better.

You can see why.

There's the Earth as normal, in its usual not-great state – holes in the ozone layer letting through dangerous radiation . . . greenhouse gases poisoning the atmosphere . . . global warming melting the polar ice caps . . . all of that.

Suddenly, most of the damage was pretty much reversed overnight. The ozone layer was back – thicker than ever. No pesky holes in it any more. The carbon dioxide levels suddenly fell, as if a hundred years of industrial pollution had been undone overnight. Acid rain became "placid" rain, calm and regular, all the sulphuric stuff squeezed out of it. And somehow, all that melting ice in the Arctic and Antarctic froze up again.

Impossible, yeah? **A MIRACLE.** No question.

Well, of course, there *were* questions. And everyone seemed to have different opinions as to what had happened.

We were still in our old, ordinary house back then.

I was woken up by the phone ringing – at five in the morning! The news was blaring from Dad's radio. It drowned out what Dad was saying on the phone, but he didn't sound happy.

He hung up and thumped down the stairs. I found him pacing around the kitchen table.

"What's going on?" I asked.

IT'S GOT TO BE GAIA, RIGHT – THE SPIRIT OF THE EARTH. SHE COULDN'T TAKE ANY MORE OF OUR MESSING STUFF UP SO HER MYSTIC SPIRIT PUT THINGS RIGHT HER OWN WAY.

THIS BIG HEAL IS GREAT NEWS FOR INDUSTRY. NOW THE PLANET'S FIXED UP, WE CAN POLLUTE MORE THAN EVER!

"I have to go to work, Tim," he said. "I've called Helen – she's coming in early to take you to school."

I shook my head. "I mean, what's going on with the planet!" The radio was still burbling with reports and facts and experts blabbing on:

"SOMETHING LIKE THIS DEFIES ALL THE NATURAL LAWS . . ."

"IT'S BIG BUSINESSES PULLING A TRICK. MUST BE . . ."

"MIRACLES NEED NO EXPLANATIONS . . ."

Dad stared into the distance.

"If something seems too good to be true, it very often is," he said.

FOUR

After the Big Heal, a lot of people thought more green miracles would happen.

Thousands gathered at the South American rainforests, waiting for Mother Nature to do her thing. They expected them to grow back overnight.

It was the same with the sea. People thought the pollution would suddenly vanish. Herbert in particular probably had his fins crossed; not for himself, being a freshwater fish, but for his ocean-dwelling brothers. He's that kind of fish – warm-hearted. Well, as warm-hearted as you can get when you're cold-blooded.

But anyway – it didn't happen.

What did happen was weirder. Wafts of strange-smelling air began to be noticed around the world.

It was a gentle, loving pong that sweet-talked your nostrils, married them in a short but moving ceremony and took them on a honeymoon to heaven. I felt sure it was the way that my ideal planet would surely smell, way out in some perfumed patch of outer space – if I could ever reach it. Even Herbert seemed excited about the smell, whizzing about in his bowl like he'd been fitted with fin jets.

"That smells **AMAZING!**" I burbled to Dad as I came down the stairs. "It's never breakfast, is it?"

"Your breakfast is cucumbers and celery chutney on toast," Dad said distantly. "This smell is something else." He was right. On both counts (unfortunately).

It soon became clear that an identical niff could be smelled all across the planet. Over land, over sea – everywhere. The only difference was that the niff was stronger the higher up you were. People in Holland, Tuvalu and Bangladesh felt a little left out, but up in the mountains of Peru the whiff was enough to charm your conk off.

No one could decide what it actually *smelled like*, though. The scent was like nothing on Earth.

And of course, the cries of "MIRACLE!" soon went up again. Surely, the Big Pong had to be a part of the Big Heal?

"This unique and joyous smell," one expert said, "is the smell of Mother Nature's healing hands."

Other experts agreed. "It's a sure sign that whatever has kick-started Earth's natural defences is still at large."

Dad did not seem happy about the smell. He got snappier and more distant than usual. Nanny Helen, on the other nostril, was delighted.

"𝒪𝑀𝒢, it's lush, isn't it?" she gushed one evening. "We'll never smell nasty fumes from cars and factories ever again."

Dad nodded and scowled. "That doesn't mean they won't be there."

"Well, it's OK, now, isn't it?" said Helen brightly. "We know the planet can heal itself—"

"It can't," Dad snapped. "That can't happen."

Helen gave him a funny look. "Er . . . it has, though."

"*Something* has happened," Dad corrected her. "Until we understand exactly what, we should be making less waste, not more."

"Why'd you have to spoil everything, Dad?" I blurted.

"You're the biggest source of *moan* pollution on the planet!"

Dad looked at me calmly. "Serious issues have to be taken seriously."

"Yeah, yeah."

I stomped away upstairs to my room and slammed the door. "Herbert, I'm sorry that fish *don't* have a three-second memory," I said (scientists have proven they remember stuff for up to five months; live with a scientist for a dad, you learn all sorts), "because I am going to have to moan to you about Dad and his super-green gloominess for the millionth time and I expect you're going to be bored . . ."

Herbert didn't seem bored. Since the Big Pong had started, he'd perked up a lot, wibbling at high speed about his bowl. But in any case, he was let off grumble duty that night.

I forgot my moaning. I was too busy staring, gobsmacked, at the weird lights whisking about the night sky, high above the traffic, through my open window.

FIVE

UFO mania!

That's what they called it.

Unidentified flying objects spotted all around the world, night after night for several weeks. Strange lights in the sky, police switchboards jammed with callers, reported sightings of dark, giant spidery creatures, tales of alien abduction . . . Nutters on TV saying the aliens were coming . . . Experts on TV saying, "Shut up, nutters". . .

Many explanations for the UFOs were put forward by all sorts of important people. Apparently, they were not alien spacecraft at all, but one of the following (decide for yourself how likely these explanations were by ticking the boxes):

this way please

FORM 27B/6 POSSIBLE EXPLANATIONS FOR UFOS PLEASE TICK ALL THAT APPLY	LIKELY	UNLIKELY	COMPLETE RUBBISH	BEYOND TOTAL LOONINESS
Atmospheric side-effects of the Big Heal				
Out of control weather balloons				
Lightning				
Unknown creatures that eat pollution and burp perfume and ozone				
Satellites falling out of orbit				
Mutant seagulls				
Odd clouds				
Hang-gliding people with enormous bums and bright trousers				
Low flying jets				
Alien warcraft				
Bats, after accidentally flying into vats of luminous paint				
Frozen poos falling from an aeroplane				

PLEASE MARK CLEARLY USING A BLACK BALLPOINT PEN

When those were your options, it was hard to know **WHAT** to think. And I didn't have anyone to ask. I had vowed never again to talk to my dad for making us move away. I tried talking to Herbert but he was more interested in showing off his new loop-the-loop trick. I had to admit that I had never seen a goldfish loop-the-loop, nor the nifty figure-of-eight he started doing soon after. It was pretty cool, if a bit weird – but there's only so many hundred times you can watch a stunt like that and feel impressed.

Nanny Helen (Helen, I mean. I know it's babyish to go on calling her "Nanny" Helen, but that's what I called her when I was little and it stuck) wasn't much better when it came to conversation:

Me: "Do you think we're being visited by aliens from outer space?"

Helen: "I don't know, Tim . . ."

Me: "They can't be clouds or jets or anything like that, can they?"

Helen: "OMG, I love clouds. They're so fluffy."

Me: "Of course, if it IS aliens and they have amazing spaceships, they probably have really bad weapons that could wipe us all out in ten seconds."

Helen: "OMG! Stop it! That's . . . OMG, that's just . . . OMG . . ."

Me: "Do you think the world will get blown up before I have to move? I'd hate to be wasting all this worry if I—"

Helen: "O!M!G! Oh . . . OMG, I don't . . . OMG! OMG, I . . . OM-GEEEEEEEEEEE . . ." etc., etc.

In the end, when Helen went home a flustered wreck, I just *had* to talk to Dad.

"Do you think the UFOs are alien spacecraft?" I asked.

"Sorry, Tim," he replied, "that's top secret."

I took a deep breath. "I'm not asking Doctor Eric Gooseheart, Head of Applied and Theoretical Quantum-Astrophysical Analysis at the Space Centre. I'm asking my dad."

Dad blinked. Then he shrugged. "I'm not sure what they are," he said. "They don't move like any type of flying craft *we* use. They don't leave any trace of exhaust gases behind either." He shook his head. "If they *are* spacecraft, I wish I knew how they worked. I've spent so many years at the Space Centre trying to . . ."

"Yes?" I broke in eagerly. "What have you been trying to do?"

He trailed off, distant again. "Never mind."

"Yes! Mind!" I cried. "Dad, you never tell me a thing. I'm sorry I'm not a genius kid like you were, but maybe if you speak slowly I'll make sense of some of it?"

"It's nothing to do with your brainpower," Dad said calmly. "Don't put yourself down. Your intelligence happens to be a little above the national average."

"Gee, thanks," I said. "What ARE those UFOs? Where do they come from?"

"Honestly, I don't know."

"OK – where do *I* come from?"

Dad stiffened like it was suddenly ten below freezing. "You're my son."

"I can't *just* be yours, can I?" I threw up my arms in frustration. "Look, I *really* need the truth, OK? And don't tell me again that the aliens just dropped me off at the Space Centre one day – or, with all these lights in the sky, I'll start worrying they've come to take me back!"

"We are not having this discussion." Dad turned and walked calmly out of the room, like he'd switched to Vulcan mode – no emotions allowed.

"Why not!" I yelled after him. "Tell me, or . . . or I'll go out and eat a cheeseburger! A massive, double Triple Bacon Royale Half-Pounder dripping with fat and dead animal juice and jammed full of cow bums and intestines and livers and a hoof . . . and . . ."

I shut up with a sigh. I was making *myself* feel sick. I heard Dad close his bedroom door. I went upstairs and slammed mine. Herbert gave me a fishy look as I stomped over to the open window and stared out into dark skies as blank as my understanding of Dad and his world.

The strange lights in the blackness would never be seen in such numbers again. The UFOs had gone. For now, anyway.

But Planet Earth's *real* troubles were just beginning . . .

SIX

In the first weeks at the Rubbish House, my ears were haunted by the humming of the special batteries sucking power from the panels above, the gurgles of our special plumbing, the thrum and hum of the turbine on the roof . . .

And the never-ending crash and banging as Dad made the most of the old, ruined windmill next to the house by installing a ma-hoosive telescope right inside it.

"Great." Staring up at the giant metal scope, which dominated the ruined mill like some conquering alien robot when it was finished, I could practically hear the tutting from the surrounding streets. "Something else for the locals to complain about."

Not for the first time, I smelled something fishy going on – and it wasn't Herbert. But that wasn't the only smell bothering me. Just lately, that sweet fragrance in the air around the world had changed into something . . . weirder.

"Can you use your telescope to find whatever's making that funny whiff?" I asked.

"Instruments at the Space Centre have recorded new molecules in the air," Dad revealed. "Whatever removed the bad stuff from Earth's atmosphere might have left something else in its place."

I was stunned. Not really by what Dad was saying, but by the way he was telling me anything at all. Amazingly, incredibly, he was **TALKING ABOUT HIS WORK**. This officially **NEVER happened!**

"You're really worried about things, aren't you, Dad?" I said quietly.

Dad quickly shook his head. "No! No way. Worry is like junk food for the mind – a greasy burger of Anxiety, or a stinking, floppy hotdog of Not Knowing What To Do," he said. "It's bad for the way you think. I prefer the crisp lettuce of Understanding a Problem and the succulent organic tomato of Knowing How to Deal With That Problem."

I sighed. My mind was hungry for the chocolate dessert of Forgetting All Your Troubles – but unfortunately it was time for the massive bowl of pease pudding and dog's muck that was my New School.

It's never easy starting at school halfway through a term. And when people found out I was the kid in the freaky house, they stared at me like I had two heads. I felt like a spaceman who'd landed on an alien world.

Over those first few weeks, I tried to fit in with minimum fuss, but no one seemed very willing to let me – least of all Fist-Face and his mates.

He's not the nicest of boys, is Fist-Face. You might think he is so-named because his face looks like a fist, but no! His face actually looks as if his neck has thrown up – not pretty! He's known as Fist-Face because his very favourite thing is punching people in the kisser. Perhaps he's jealous of normal-faced people who don't look like their ears stepped in something.

Anyway, if anyone was seen talking to me, Fist-Face gave them a dead arm and promised that something more serious would die too if they ever spoke to me again. Which wasn't great.

Like the rising smell of *yuk* in the air, things were starting to stink a little more with every passing day – for both me and the world at large.

I told Dad about the bullying. I'm not sure he was really listening.

"Tim, my worries are kind of bigger, planet-Earth kind of worries."

"Oh." In the battle between picked-on son and picked-on planet, I knew Earth would always win in Dad's eyes.

"Er . . ." Dad must've realised what he'd said. "Your worries are important too, of course."

"Yeah. Thanks, Dad." I stuffed my hands in my pockets. "That doesn't make me feel like poo at all."

"Remember, Tim, we recycle poo in this house. You may feel like you're being flushed down life's toilet, but you will re-emerge from fate's sewer in a stronger and more useful state."

I blinked. "Dad, I think that was, like, the worst inspirational speech in the history of the world."

But he was already back looking through his 'scope, in a world – or a universe – of his own.

(VIEW THROUGH TELESCOPE) (WOW, SO EXCITING)

SEVEN

It turned out Dad had done something nice – he'd invited Nanny Helen (Helen! Just Helen!) round for dinner that night as a treat. It had been three weeks since we'd said goodbye. I'd really missed her.

Dad said he had missed her too, but he seemed distracted that night. The wind-up radio chattered away as he prepared his famous (and not for good reasons) yellow rice sushi.

". . . the change in the air's scent has been noticed all over the planet," the radio voice announced. "Once described as 'the gentle perfume of Mother Nature's healing hands', critics in mountainous Peru are today calling it 'more like the nasty niff of Mother Nature's sweaty armpits . . .'"

"It's hard to describe properly, isn't it?" Dad mused.

"What?" I smiled cheekily at Helen. "How disgusting

your sushi is?"

"The smell in the air," Dad said seriously. "To me, it smells like musty sheets washed in lemon juice and left to dry in an abandoned Turkish market surrounded by forest fires. What about you, Helen?"

"Oh! Er . . . um . . . I can't think!" Helen waved her hands in front of her face as if she needed to cool down. "Your go, Tim."

I thought hard for ages. Then I shrugged. "I can only think of something really dumb."

"Go on," said Dad.

"Well . . . I have this funny idea." I shrugged again. "Just cos we're human beings, we think everything on the planet was put there for us. So we moan about this smell – but maybe other animals smell it differently."

Helen grinned. "You mean we should ask Herbert what he thinks of it?"

"Scents disperse more slowly in water than in air," Dad began seriously, "and they are important to fish. Smells help them identify environments and individuals and—"

"Yeah, OK, Dad." I didn't want him hijacking my little effort so soon. "I just mean that . . . well, everyone knows that dung pongs and it's horrible, right? But a dung beetle must love that smell, cos it eats dung, and rolls it up into balls, and lives off it."

Helen almost choked on her yellow rice and seaweed. "Huh? You lost me."

"Dungballs?" Dad was staring into space like he was in a trance. "*Dungballs* . . . **DUNGBALLS!**"

"Oh, no, Eric!" said Helen. "I wouldn't say your sushi was that bad!"

We all laughed. Even Dad smiled. This was turning out to be a pretty good night.

"Right, my turn," said Helen. "OK, then – I reckon this whiff smells like old socks boiled in cocoa that's gone off a bit, right, then left in the spare room of my new family's house, which – OMG – it really reeks, I'm telling you . . ."

"Your new family?" I squeaked.

Suddenly this was NOT pretty good. It was ugly bad.

"New kids to look after, yeah . . . Starting next

week." Helen smiled sadly. "Course, they won't be as nice as you, Tim! But, well, you know . . ." She glanced at my dad. "A girl's got to eat."

I glared at my dad. Had he known about this?

But Dad looked pale, still staring into the distance. Still muttering about dungballs.

EIGHT

I hope you'll agree, I had one or two pretty pongy problems.

But, it soon turned out, some people had things even worse.

There was once a village called Tradnensky. Heard of it? Tradnensky stood for over three hundred years in the snowy wilds of Russian Siberia, three time zones and two thousand miles east of Moscow.

A lot of people lived there – farmers and fishers and old folk, mainly. The biggest problem they had to deal with was the cost of ammo for their rifles, which made hunting kind of expensive.

Then one afternoon in May – just a couple of days after Not-Nanny-Just-Helen had dropped her bombshell – an insane rush of yellow goo fell from the sky and the entire place was swept clean away.

Or rather, it was swept *messy* away.

"It was like a tidal wave, only from out of the sky," one shocked eyewitness said. "And it was yellow. And it stank."

Houses fell apart in the sudden flood. Cars were crushed like old cans. Belongings were washed away in the dark, sticky torrents until they dissolved or washed up in the snow. Dozens of lakes in the area turned yellow. Thousands of fish were finished off in moments – they floated to the surface and burst into flames.

The news footage kept showing a wide-eyed Siberian girl, who spoke of the catastrophe with a haunting eloquence (and English subtitles):

"Mother Nature has made the sky sick on us! She says, 'I get you! Boom, you're going down, human beings, she says! Boom, boom, I'm Mother Gangster now. Bye-bye human rubbish on my skin! I pop a cap in yo butt! Yeah! BOOM!'"

I woke up the next day and I had overslept. Massively.

It was ten in the morning and school was going on without me.

Why hadn't Dad woken me?

I heard him on the phone, downstairs.

"I've been warning you that something like this would happen." His voice was quiet and very serious – this was the equivalent of a normal human shouting his bum off, and three-and-a-half times as scary. "I told you about the particles in the air forming a kind of code, and I warned you the invisible sightings were real. Well, now you **HAVE** to believe me . . . No! The government can cover up the evidence but we must make the hyper-beam project a new priority . . . The governments of the world **HAVE TO** meet this threat . . . Yes, I **WILL** go public on this if I have to . . ."

Dad hung up at last, and cold-sweat chills corkscrewed down my spine. I didn't know what was going on, but Maths, PE and a dead arm from Fist-Face suddenly seemed incredibly appealing.

I got dressed and went downstairs. The news was still full of the explosive downpour in Siberia. "Samples of the yellow downpour have been gathered at last, but so far, they have experts stumped. The substance resists all attempts at analysis . . ."

"Hello, Tim," said Dad calmly.

"I'm late for school." I'm pretty good at stating the obvious. "Really late."

"That's OK. I think you should leave school anyway."

I blinked. "What?"

He shrugged. "I don't believe there's much point in your going any more."

"WHAT?"

"I'm not going to go to work, either. We'll stay home together. OK?"

"OK . . ."A chill buzzed through me. "Uh, Dad? What do you think the yellow stuff is?"

"I'm not sure. But I don't think this incident will be the only one. I think there's more to come."

"Why?" I asked.

But Dad didn't answer, because the breaking news on the TV was that in Europe, half of Luxembourg had been buried under a colossal silver blanket that had fallen out of the sky.

"We're in trouble," said Dad.

NINE

SKY FALLS IN ON LUXEMBOURG.

That's what one newspaper said.

LUXEMBOURG BURIED BY CLOTH FROM SPACE,

said another.

BAD LUCK-SEMBOURG IN EURO-SQUELCH!

said yet another.

(Although Dad didn't buy that one.)

FREAK EVENT SMOTHERS CITY,

said one of the boring, serious newspapers.

The Big Blanket, as it soon became known, wasn't *really* a blanket – there was no stitching, and it couldn't have been made by any factory on Earth.

The Big Blanket had flattened several buildings and where its edges trailed the ground, cars had crashed into it. Eyewitnesses described it as "definitely metal, only watery and mixed with smoke". Or, "shiny with ripples . . . Not Ripples like the chocolate bar – I mean like rippling liquid . . . only solid". Or, "it was roughly smooth and narrowly thick and soaking wet except when you touched it, when it tingled dryly". No one seemed able to actually describe it.

Dad nodded to himself. "Knew it! Something else that defies analysis."

I looked at Dad. "You know that time I said the smell in the air was like something maybe not meant for human noses?"

"Dungball day," Dad remembered.

"Yeah, well . . . that's a bit like this stuff. It can't be understood properly by any of our senses. Like it's . . . it's . . ."

"Alien?" Dad looked at me coolly. "Yes. I think this stuff is alien too."

I squeaked like a field mouse in the beak of an owl. "You do?"

He nodded.

"You think aliens are real?"

"I know they are, Tim," he said quietly. "Some have visited our world . . . and some have stayed."

I was gobsmacked. Well, actually I was gob-struck-with-a-thermonuclear-warhead. Proper, actual, **ALIENS?** Did that mean there really was something to Dad's age-old tale I'd been dropped on his doorstep from outer space? I wanted to say something, but the words shrivelled on my tongue.

"These latest UFOs have been very different, though," Dad went on. "An unknown race that take 'alien' to a whole other level." It was almost as if he'd forgotten I was there, and just needed to let things out. "The particles are like nothing our science has ever discovered. It may be that what we think of as a 'smell' is something very different to alien senses."

Wow, I thought. "You mean, to them, the smell could actually be a taste? Or something they can see?"

Dad started at the sound of my voice. "Er . . . yes,

like a pattern. A kind of code, if you like. Delivered into the air somehow . . . a message most likely for our attention."

That was a hard one to get my head around perhaps. (Or to get my nose around, if I was an alien.) "A code or a message . . . saying what?"

"I have no idea," Dad admitted. "I want to find out, but the Space Centre don't believe my theories. They think I've gone bonkers."

"Have you?"

"Let's hope so."

A long, scary, wondering moment passed between us at the approximate speed of a drugged tortoise doing forward rolls through treacle.

"Is this why you don't want me to go to school?" I managed to say at last. "You're worried about me?"

"Er, well, a bit," said Dad unconvincingly. "Actually, I need you home to help with my experiments here."

I frowned. "But I'm no use at science."

"Don't worry. I'll show you what to do," Dad said. "It might even be fun!"

It wasn't, of course.

Unless your idea of fun is shivering out in the back garden all night every night for a **(BORING!)** week, taking spectrographic weirdographs through a telescope at intervals of precisely forty-two seconds.

To stop me falling asleep in the early hours, Dad kept me up by calling me on a walkie-talkie. **BLEEP-BLEEP! SQUAWK!** it blared, making me jump. He was working in the lounge. Not that you could do much lounging there now he'd set up all these big machines to analyse every iota of the mysterious particles. He needed my scans to keep the machines number crunching; it was the only way to work out what the code might be saying.

It took less effort to work out what the *neighbours* were saying. Between all the squawks and bleeps and the whoosh of the windmill's sails and the groaning **THRUMMM** of the solar batteries trying to make enough electricity to cope with everything day and night, the Rubbish House was no longer just an eyesore. It had become an *earsore* too.

"If we'd known you noisy beggars were moving in we'd have sold up and cleared off!" said the neighbours to our left.

And as the days passed with no more weird indescribable things dropping from the sky, I wondered if maybe the danger was past. Then I began to wonder if it had ever existed.

What if it turned out Dad *had* gone crazy? He might get arrested. I might have to go to a children's home. Herbert would go back to a pet shop (or into training for the Loopy Fish Olympics).

Even the Rubbish House and nights spent slaving over a hot weirdoscope would be better than that.

TEN

The school phoned a couple of times, but Dad refused to pick up. He'd told the head that I was taking a leave of absence for the foreseeable future. He wasn't prepared to waste any more time or mind power on arguing the toss with "small-minded officials".

I wondered if the head would send someone round to talk to us, like social services, or the police.

In fact, a couple of people did come to call. But the head had nothing to do with it . . .

I'd been sleeping most of the day after yet another staggeringly dull and noisy night wrapped up in the windmill, working the telescope. When I woke up, stiff and sore around four o'clock in the afternoon, I hoped that Dad would crack his code soon. Or just crack up, if he had to, so he could start getting better and I could start sleeping and acting normally again.

BONG! The doorbell rang. I waited for Dad to open the door. He didn't.

"Dad?" I called. Nothing.

I got up in my pyjamas and looked in Dad's room. Empty.

BONG! The doorbell chimed again. Who could be calling?

In my half-awake stumble down the stairs I remembered coming home from school in the old days to Not-Nanny-Just-Helen. I always used to roll my eyes, because the moment she answered the door she would squeal, *"OMGeeeeeeeee!"* and grab me in a hug. It had always seemed a bit of an overreaction considering I came home at the same time every day. Now, I missed her and the hugs horribly.

Through the glass panel of the door, it looked like someone was waiting with their arms open now. It's Helen, I thought, still in my daze. Helen! I scrabbled at the bolts and threw open the door . . .

To find Darren "Fist-Face" Gilbert stepping forward, arms reaching out to grab me.

"Hiding away in your freak-hole, Goosefart?" he sneered.

I yelped, suddenly wide awake. On the drive behind Fist-Face I saw his oversized chief thug, Lardy, and a crowd of kids from school. From the gloating grins on their faces I guessed they weren't members of the Timothy Gooseheart fan club.

I slammed the door and jumped backwards. Fist-Face banged on the door. "Chicken! Open up!"

"Er, no!" I said wittily. My heart had grown fists and was thumping my ribcage like a heavyweight. "My Dad's upstairs. He'll get you."

"We saw your dad go out ages ago, loser," Lardy informed me.

"I had a whole thing going against you, Goosefart!" Fist-Face shouted. "Then you pushed off before we got to the best part – where I hammer you in front of the whole school. So now I've brought the show to *you* . . ."

He was banging on the door, and I knew that if I opened it I would be pulverised.

Which left the *back* door as my only option. Maybe I could sneak out through the kitchen, climb over next door's fence and give Fist-Face and Lardy the slip? Although with all the noise we'd been making, if the neighbours caught me they'd probably hand me over.

Fraught with danger though it was, it was the only plan I had.

It might even have worked.

Except that as I sprinted into the kitchen, I found the door was already open – and blocked by a burly guy in a hazard suit and gas mask, pointing a gun straight at me.

Not, like, a cop's popgun or something.

This looked like a *space* gun.

ELEVEN

Nothing I can write now could capture the terror I felt at that moment. But my feet gave a fair impression by spinning me round and propelling me back to the front door at about a million miles per hour.

My fingers tore at the front latch – and Fist-Face kicked the door open. It slammed into me, knocking me sideways against the hall wall. I sank down, stunned.

"Got you!" Fist-Face bellowed, stomping inside – where he almost collided with Hazard-Suit Man. And suddenly, Fist-Face was the one staring down the barrel of a gun.

He gave a high-pitched *cheep!* like a baby bird, wet himself dramatically and threw a wild punch at the intruder – all at the same time. Whatever else you might say about Fist-Face, he can multitask.

The intruder took the blow to the face – or rather, to the extremely solid gas mask – and went down.

Fist-Face yelled and shook his knuckles – which had most likely broken on the mask's hard plastic. Sobbing, he staggered outside. After staring in mystified horror at the intruder on the floor, I hauled myself up and followed Fist-Face out into sunlight.

In my fright I'd forgotten the watching crowd from school – and wow, were they ever watching now. They'd come to see me get slaughtered by the school bully; what they wound up seeing was the school bully bursting out of my house in soaked trousers, holding his swollen fist and racing from sight like a cat with a firework up its bum.

"Huh?" Lardy pointed in consternation. "Goosefart made Fist-Face wet himself?" The stunned crowd burst into gales of laughter.

"Get away!" I shouted at them, checking behind me that the intruder was still down. "Get out of here! Just go!"

Spotting, I guess, that I had left Fist-Face wee-soaked, wee-*ping* and running for his life, Lardy scarpered and the crowd followed him, shaking their heads, excited, well-entertained. "Who'd have thought Goosefart was so tough?" one girl said.

You have no idea, I thought.

I wanted to sprint after them, as shock gave way to panic. What had the intruder been up to in the house? Why the gas mask as well as the gun? What did he want? What was I doing even hanging around here when the intruder could get up any moment and shoot me in two seconds flat?

I was about to bolt for it when I realised a distant, whirring drone had been slowly getting louder. What was the cause? Like a celestial "DUH!" aimed squarely at me, a shadow swooped overhead with a deafening din. The savage rush of the rotor rhythm whirled hard through my head, and turned the air into a solid thing that knocked me to the ground.

I rolled over, shielded my eyes and ears from the maelstrom of wind and grit and noise and found myself staring up at a helicopter coming in to land.

A. Hell. Eee. Cop. Ter. Touching down in my front garden!

Our noise-hating neighbours would be running for the hills (or at least the nearest estate agents).

The copter had a big glass dome around the cockpit, like Herbert's bowl. But there was no busy little fish to be seen here. Only a pilot wearing a mask and hazard suit like the intruder's identical twin . . .

And my father, seated beside him.

"Dad!" I yelled, scrambling up as the crescendo of wind and rotors finally began to wind down. But Dad didn't hear. His eyes were closed.

There was movement behind me. I saw the intruder, waving his sci-fi gun, back on his feet. He knocked me off mine with a squeeze of his trigger. PHUT! I felt cold for a second. A little fluffy dart was suddenly sticking out of my arm.

Then the world went dark, like I was lost in space. Stars were spinning round my head. I couldn't help but wonder which planets circled them, and if those bloated, spidery creatures the UFO nuts said they'd seen might live there.

So much for my last thoughts before I blacked out completely.

TWELVE

I woke up and I was on a plane.

A big flashy plane, full of gorillas with guns. Not real gorillas. Men who looked quite like gorillas. (Only they had shaved. Or someone had shaved for them. More gorillas, with shaving kits, maybe? I don't know.)

I turned to find Dad seated opposite. An American man in a smart grey suit – he didn't have a gun, but looked to be bossing round the ones who did – was quietly explaining that Dad was **NEEDED**. Lots of experts from around the world were **NEEDED** to work on the big problems that faced our little planet.

"So you were right, Dad," I whispered. "The Earth is in trouble."

"And then some," said The Suit.

Through the window there was nothing to see but

endless grey ocean. "Where are we going?" Dad demanded.

The Suit's lips twitched. "You'll see."

"Why couldn't you just *ask* me if I'd come with you?" Dad was shaking, but I think more with anger than fear. "Why resort to violence? Why *shoot* us both with tranquilliser darts? Why kidnap us?"

"We also blew up your house," The Suit said calmly.

Dad and I chorused beautifully: **"WHAT?!"**

"That's our cover story for your disappearance. Locals will believe our helicopter was an air ambulance—"

"Herbert!" I shouted.

The Suit gestured that I should stay calm. "Your fish is OK – he's stowed in the cargo hold with some of your stuff. Relax."

"*Relax?*" Dad's voice had dropped to its iciest whisper. **"You BLEW UP OUR HOME?"**

"The way things are, we can't afford to do things nicey-nicey," said The Suit. "The future of the world needs your mind working on the problem in our way, in our space, and to our schedule."

Me and Dad just stared at each other, shocked and scared. The Rubbish House . . . blown apart . . .

"Sorry you had to be brought into this, kid." The Suit was looking at me. "It's your dad we need, but we couldn't just leave you behind."

"I can look after myself," I lied, rubbishly.

"We didn't bring you along out of the kindness of our hearts. You'll be joining the other child hostages."

Me and Dad swapped incredulous looks. I think mine was slightly better than his; I was the child-hostage-in-training after all. Before we could properly kick off with the scandalised protests, The Suit jumped in:

"Yes, I said 'hostages'. As in, someone held prisoner by a powerful captor until the captor's demands are met." He patted me on the head. "You see, your dad really has to cooperate with us one hundred per cent. On the time scale we think we've got, there's no other way." The Suit looked straight at Dad. "You get me, Professor Gooseheart?"

Dad looked away and nodded. "I get you."

I said nothing, frozen solid with sheer ULP.

The Suit shut his eyes and pretended to go to sleep.

Hours rolled resentfully by. Somebody brought pieces of pizza, which no one ate. I looked out of the window, but now we were flying over a bare expanse of snow. There was nothing but bright icy wilderness to look at.

Dad stared out the window then slumped into the empty seat beside me, ashen-faced. "Dungballs," he said.

I groaned. "Not this again!"

"A dung beetle believes he owns his dungball," Dad went on. "He crawls all over it, fights for it, consumes it, steers it wherever he likes. But the beetle doesn't really own a thing. He just came along, found the dung and pinched it."

I felt a prickling shiver blizzard through me as I finally got what he was driving at. "You mean . . . planet Earth is like the dungball, and humans are like the beetles?"

"We're top of the food chain, so we think we own the lot." Dad shook his head. "But what if somebody else was here first . . . ?"

Just at that moment, I realised that I *could* see

something in that never-ending whiteness far below: a gigantic sunken shape in the snow, roughly circular, with smaller ovals scattered all around it. A long way ahead, I could see a similar marking. And another beyond that. The quiet plane erupted into panicked chatter as others saw what I had seen.

Those markings in the snow were like footprints. Not human footprints.

Giant. ALIEN. FOOTPRINTS.

Dad stared past me, out of the window, and as he spoke again my blood ran cold: "Yes, what if someone owned our planet, way before humans even existed? And . . . what if they've come back?"

PART TWO

Please, please, please, please,
please, please, please, please,
please, please, please, please,
please, please, please, please,
please, please, please, please,
please, please, please, please,
please, please, please, please,
please, please, please, please,
please, please, please, please,
please, please, please, please,
please, please, please, please,
please, please, please, please,
please, please, please, please,
please, please, please, please,
please, please, please, please,
please, please, please, please,
please, please, please, please,
please, please, please, please,
PLEASE
let us all live long enough
for there to be a **PART THREE**

(please?)

THIRTEEN

(What a happy number to kick off **PART TWO**)

So. That was then, this is now. And now, I'm here.

Where is here, you might ask? (I only said *might*. I'm not accusing you.) "Here" is a top-secret scientific base dug into the permafrost of the north polar ice cap – a massive underground complex where tons of weird, unbelievable and highly dangerous research is carried out.

I've decided that, if the planet ever gets through this, I am definitely going to make a book about it. If anything happens to me, the proof will all be here, written down.

Mind you, I'm fairly convinced that secret-agent types will *know* I've written it down and if I try to tell you too much about it I'll probably be censored by the CENSORED THIS IS SECRET , particularly if it's read by the guy in charge, General NO WAY, NOT ON YOUR NELLY of the United States NO–NO who is currently commander-in-chief of the STOP THAT organisation, set up to protect Earth from aliens – an organisation apparently known as the THIS IS NONE OF YOUR BUSINESS

So if I just call it the **Super-Secret Base For Protecting Earth That Doesn't Really Exist, I'm Making It All Up Honestly So Don't Worry About It**, that will do for now.

Anyway, soon after our plane flew past the freaky footprints, we looked set to fly straight into the side of a mountain.

That was nice.

There was me, hair on end, gripping the seat in front and shouting, **"NOOOOOOOOOOOOO OOOOOOOOOOOOOOOOOOOO OOOO!!!! HELPMESOMEONE IDON'TWANTTODIEEEEEEE EEEEEEEEEEE!!!!!"** when suddenly a secret heated airstrip rose up from the snowy wastes all around and we landed with barely a bump.

Which was good from a staying alive point of view, but kind of embarrassing after all the fuss I'd made.

Once we landed, the airstrip dropped slowly down into the snow, taking us into some kind of incredible **Super-Secret Base For Protecting Earth That Doesn't Really Exist, I'm Making It All Up Honestly So Don't Worry About It**. I stared out of the window at the new, subterranean world around me. A huge hangar had been carved out of the well-lit rock. Military men and women bustled about small aircraft, rockets and satellites, like visitors to an underground museum.

The Suit and his gorillas bundled me and Dad outside and into the noise and kerfuffle. The yukky smell was just the same down here – the alien whiff-code, or whatever it was, was truly global.

"Have our new guests shown to their rooms," said The Suit. "Then escort Dr Gooseheart to Meeting Room One."

"What about Tim?" asked Dad.

"He'll be taken care of," said The Suit.

Did he mean "taken care of" as in "we'll give him a nice warm drink and a comic and then tuck him into bed so he can have a lovely snooze"? Or as in, "we'll stick him in a sack, kick him about a bit, fire machineguns at him, sling his body in a furnace and bury his ashes outside in the ice so you'll never see him again"?

At that time, I almost didn't mind which. I was so scared and, like, **WHOA!** after all that had happened and was continuing to happen, I just wanted to close my eyes and hide.

In a daunted daze, I took in my surroundings: big tunnels chewed out of the rock by machines, big metal slabs for doors with big **KEEP OUT** signs daubed in scary red paint, big rooms for big meetings with big scientists guarded by big soldiers.

And little me feeling as small as a dung beetle.

A burly black soldier named Sergeant Katzburger showed us to our adjoining rooms. She might be the most miserable person I have ever met. She has a mohawk like Mr T with longer bits at the back, and her face always has this kind of hangdog expression. Which is a bit weird when your name sounds like "cat burger". You'd think it would be a dog's favourite thing.

Anyway, our rooms were more like prison cells, with bare breeze-block walls, grey floor tiles, camp beds, a toilet and a sink.

"There," she said, in the deepest American accent I've ever heard. "Your home from home."

In normal circumstances, if you were on holiday and you'd travelled about 2500 miles only to find yourself in a room like ours, you'd probably complain to the manager. Unfortunately, the manager had already drugged us and kidnapped us so he/she probably figured complaints about accommodation would come some way down the list – and he/she was right. That first day I arrived I was just glad I had any sort of a bed, mainly as I planned to hide under it.

At least it was ready-built, unlike the Rubbish House the first day I arrived there.

I really couldn't believe it.

I'd never much liked that place (remember page 10?), but to think of it in flames and pieces . . . What would the guys at school make of that? Would Fist-Face become prime suspect in the case of our violent exit from the community, and go to prison for years? That would be something, anyway . . .

A young soldier stuck his head round the door while squinting at a blue clipboard. "Time to go, Doc Gooseheart. You got a meeting in Weird Science Group Two."

Dad looked at me forlornly. "Take care, Tim. I'm sure I won't be long."

"Round here you can't be sure about anything," said Sergeant Katzburger gruffly. "You'll probably be ages. Hours. Days, even." As Dad was escorted away by the clipboard guy, I waved as best I could with my hand shaking.

"Where's Herbert?" I asked Katzburger.

"The goldfish will follow on shortly," she said, and I imagined Herbert pursuing us mysteriously through the air (after his many mega-moves lately, it wouldn't have surprised me that much). "Meantime, I'll get someone to take you to the Crèche."

I frowned. "Huh? Crèche as in, for little kids?"

"No," she said flatly. "Round here, nothing's as it should be. You'll see." Then she looked at my jumble-sale clothes disapprovingly and nodded to a holdall. "We brought some of your clothes here, if you want to change."

"How thoughtful of you to shoot me with a tranquilliser dart so I didn't have to pack them myself," I should've said – but of course I just nodded dumbly.

"You'll be all right, kid," Katzburger went on. "Well, probably . . . possibly . . ." She sucked in her cheeks. "You *might* be all right. If you watch out for those other weirdo kids, and if you . . . well . . ." She sighed. "Look, you probably won't be all right, to be honest. But try not to think about it. That's what I do." She walked out the door and shot one last, hangdog look back at me. "It doesn't work, but I keep trying. So long, kid."

Yeah, so long, I thought. As she closed the door, I felt suddenly and horribly alone.

I banged on the door. No reply. I opened it, but Sergeant Katzburger wasn't there. Of course, she'd gone – I didn't need a guard or anything. It wasn't like I could escape anywhere, was it? Where would I go?

HMM, THINK I'LL JUST ABANDON DAD, NIP OUTSIDE AND FREEZE TO DEATH . . . GET MAULED BY A POLAR BEAR . . . BE PECKED BY A KILLER PENGUIN . . . WHILE HOPING A FRIENDLY SNOWPLOUGH TAXI DRIVER WITH A VERY LARGE PETROL TANK TRUNDLES BY?

TAXI

No, this **Super-Secret Base For Protecting Earth That Doesn't Really Exist, I'm Making It All Up Honestly So Don't Worry About It** was home for the foreseeable future.

How long would that be?

Did the world even **HAVE** a future?

I closed the door and sat on the camp bed. I didn't know whether to shout or scream or cry or go **OO-OO-AH-AHHHH** like a chimp or bang my head against the wall or use the toilet or stare at the battered holdall in the corner of the room which had started moving like there was something inside it or shout **"HELP, HELP, I AM A PRISONER IN A SUPER-SECRET BASE FOR PROTECTING EARTH THAT DOESN'T REALLY EXIST, I'M MAKING IT ALL UP HONESTLY SO DON'T WORRY ABOUT IT"** or start running in a circle or . . .

Hang on – the holdall was moving like there was something **INSIDE** it?

What?

WHAT?

WHAAAAAAAAAAT—?

Suddenly, with a loud, rude, unzipping sound, a horrible, wrinkly head burst out from the battered leather bag like a slimy green rugby ball.

THERE WAS AN **ALIEN** IN MY HOLDALL!

FOURTEEN

I sat frozen on the bed. Staring.

Three dark eyes stared back and winked at me in sequence.

There was a living creature in my holdall. It was like nothing on Earth.

You might remember this bit from the start of the book. I threw it in there to kind of get your attention and draw you into the story. Pretty cool stylistic device, huh?

I also threw it in because your first meeting with an ALIEN takes time to get over. And now you've had about 71 pages. See? I'm good to you.

Alien.

Alien? Alien! Alien; alien. Alien: A:L.I;E-N, a I i e n, alien. Alien— @lien . . .

Dad said aliens were real . . . that some had visited

and stayed.

As Helen would say, O.M.GEEEEEEE!

Little green men – that's often how the UFO-spotters describe creatures from space, isn't it? That's the image that stuck. Well, this little "man" was very green. And boy, was he ugly.

His three eyes were probably the most normal thing about him. His ears looked like noses – which wasn't surprising because in fact, they *were* noses, one either side of his head. And where a nose should be there was something like an ear. And hanging between those noses, pitched beneath the ear like a wide, toothy hammock, was the creature's mouth, stretched open in a weird grin . . .

"Hello!" said the little green man in a funny, gruff voice. "Hello!"

I opened my mouth but no sound could sneak out. I wanted to run, but my limbs had locked solid.

"Hello, clothes!" The alien lifted out some of my T-shirts and trousers from the holdall, gripping them with long, sticky fingers. "Clothes! Hello. Hello!"

"Wh . . ." I began; a promising start, I trust you'll

agree. "Wh . . . Wha . . . What . . . ?"

"RUBBISH!" The alien tossed the clothes away. "Lame! Hello?!"

I tried again: "What . . . are . . . you . . . ?"

"What am I WEARING?" Suddenly he jumped out of the bag and landed by the door, blocking my way out. "Hello? See! Hello!"

Now I could see he really was a little green man – about the same size as a penguin. His slimy lump of a body was badly concealed beneath an old tweed waistcoat. A gold medallion hung around his neck. His big four-fingered hands were on his hips. Stumpy, kneeless legs poked out from a pair of football shorts, ending in big flippery feet squashed into a pair of flip-flops. But why am I bothering to describe it when you can just look at a picture?

LITTLE
Gx

Before I could get any further with my attempts to speak, the alien spoke again: "I'm Little G!"

"You're . . ."

"Little G!" He held up his medallion like a cop showing ID. "Hello! Little G! I'm not wearing none of your rubbish clothes!"

"You . . . were stealing my clothes!" I said dumbly.

"NO! Stuff them in the toilet!" Then Little G's three eyes widened and he suddenly gave a weird, throaty cry, like he'd stepped on something. "You! You . . . are the one! The one who WILL!"

It was a good thing I'd lost the power to talk as I wasn't sure what to say to that in any case. "Um . . . will what?"

"Spaceboy." The alien threw open his long arms. "Give me a hug."

"Huh?"

"Hug, spaceboy!"

I took a step back. "What?"

"Hello! Hug." He clapped, as if I were a puppy and he was trying to get my attention. "You and Little G. Right now. Hug."

"Why did you call me 'spaceboy'?"

"GIVE ME A HUG!" Little G sped towards me, waddling like a penguin in his flip-flops. I backed away into the bathroom and climbed on top of the toilet. "Get away from me!"

But the weirdo alien wasn't giving up. "Hug! Hug! Hello! Hug! You the one who will! I smell the tongue." He waved his arms, reaching out to grab me. **"The TONGUE! THE TONNNNNNNNNNGUE!!!"**

FIFTEEN

"Leave me alone!" I yelled, and I jumped through the air, right over Little G's head. I landed nimbly and ran for the door – which suddenly opened, clonking me in the face.

"OWW!" I fell back onto the bed. Next moment, I felt Little G's long, sticky arms wrap around me.

"Mmmmm." Little G snuggled his sticky green face against my cheek. "Hug, spaceboy. Fly high, fly high! Mmm, tongue! I can smell it!"

"Stop smelling my tongue," I cried. "Somebody save meeeeeee!"

"Oh, man," came a girl's voice from the doorway. "Uh, Little G? I think the new kid would like you to let him go now."

"He the one, Elodie! Spaceboy! Hello!"

"Don't think so, G." She sounded American to me,

but with a funny accent. "Go on, now. Scoot."

"Scoot?" Looking kind of hurt, Little G let go of me and waddled away, out of the room. "I smell the tongue! Bye-bye, spaceboy-one. Bye-bye, Elodie!" He walked away – then suddenly came back and attempted a clumsy high five with Elodie before leaving again. "Bye! See you soon! Byeeee!"

I was left shivering on the bed, looking at this Elodie girl – a girl around my own age with freckles and dark hair like mine only longer.

"So, I guess you're gonna have some questions," said Elodie, folding her arms.

"Yes," I said weakly.

"Well, do you mind if we run through them real fast? I've been mentally calculating some seriously mental calculations and I don't want to forget my place before I get to the Crèche. Do me a favour, eh? Remember seven-three-nine-seven-seven-point-three."

I gulped. "Seven . . . three . . . ?"

"Now, things you need to know – am I American? No, I'm from Ontario. That's in Canada. Call me

American and I'll break your face."

"Um . . . OK." I was still reeling from my close encounter with the little green man who'd just been chasing me. "Listen, who—?"

"Who is my mother?" Elodie smiled, approvingly. "My mother is the famous scientist Hannah-Anna Hongananner. You've heard of her, of course."

"No."

"**WHAT?** Where've you been, kid? You've never heard of the Hongananner Theory of Quantum Scatter?"

"No."

"The Hongananner Atomic Code-Splitting Engine?"

"No."

"The Hongananner Theory of the Emission of Titulus-Sprinkle Molecules in Ambient Space?"

"Yes."

"Really?"

"NO!" I cried. "Now, never mind all that, what about—"

"What about you. Uh-huh." Elodie nodded. "Time out from your questions – I got one of my own.

What's your name?"

"Tim," I replied, not unreasonably. "And I'm with my dad, he's a space genius. But—"

"Yeah? Who is he?"

"Look, never mind all that, right now!" I insisted. "You're meant to be answering my questions. What did I just meet in here—?"

"Oh, Little G?" Elodie lowered one eyebrow and raised the other. "Crashed on Earth in the Mojave desert in Southern California, years back. Only survivor. Seems kind of dumb. US military got him; they're keeping him around until the military perfect their brain-drain device to suck out any secret know-how he may have hidden away in there. These guys don't play around. Too much at stake, protectors of the world, blah blah blah."

I opened my mouth to butt in. "Er—"

"OK, next question," Elodie went on forcefully. "You're thinking, is Little G anything to do with the Giant Extra-Terrestrials who left those big footprints outside? Answer: no, he's from a totally different galaxy. But studying his native language has helped my mum and her team translate a little of the GETs' smell-code. My mum, your dad, all the others, they're now part of a super-brainy think tank working on how to sort out the Alien Problem."

"Um—?"

"I guess you're wondering what's next for you now, eh?" Elodie nodded sympathetically. "Well, you're gonna join us in the Crèche, where us hostage kids can pass time while our genius scientist parents work their butts off. But with a little not-always-willing help from Sergeant Katzburger, we've made the Crèche into something a bit more hardcore." She leaned against the side of the doorway. "Now, what was that number I told you to remember?"

I coughed awkwardly. "Three-something?"

Elodie blinked. Then she smiled sympathetically. "I get it. Too much information for your brain in one hit. Sorry, kid. I just assumed you'd be a brainiac like the rest of us."

I frowned. "Huh?"

"Cle-ver peo-ple," Elodie intoned slowly. "Don't worry. Why not come with me to the Crèche and meet the other inmates? You may as well." She paused and half smiled. "Unless you'd rather call back Little G for a smooch?"

I was at her side in a moment. Safety in numbers, right? That's what I thought.

And of course, I was wrong.

SIXTEEN

I followed Elodie through the well-lit tunnels. She was muttering under her breath – big numbers by the sound of it. My head was spinning. First I'd seen evidence of alien life in massive footprint form. Then I'd seen it in the flesh. And it had smelled my tongue. Ugh! Its appearance here threw a freaky new spin on Dad's tall tale of aliens dropping me on the doorstep.

"Little G called me 'the one'," I said. "What did he mean by that?"

Elodie stopped counting and shrugged. "He probably just means there's one of you. His ship gave up some cool pointers for the secret experimental space travel programme they're working on here, and they hoped Little G would show them how to work it. But he seems kind of useless with technology.

Prefers clothes. Anyways, you want to know what the G stands for, right?"

"Er—"

"Well, who knows? It's just what he calls himself. Don't worry about G – he's harmless. And kind of dim." She paused. "But don't worry, I'm sure that's not why he seems to like you so much."

"Thanks," I muttered. "If any alien has to take an interest in me, I'd sooner it's him and not one of those Giant Extra-Terrestrials. How big must they be to leave such massive great footprints in the snow?"

"Maybe a thousand metres tall?" said Elodie. "The latest theory is that the GETs can change their physical state from solid to weightless and back again. Otherwise there'd be prints all over the place. Same with their spaceships – that's why no one's seen any trace that they've landed."

"If they're that big, they could park on a mountain and hop down to Earth like we jump off a bus," I said, trying to get my head round it. "But if big fat aliens—"

"No one said they were chubby."

"—are walking about the place, how come no one's seen them?"

"They can hide themselves. Maybe on purpose . . . Maybe because they're so alien, our eyes kind of reject them." Elodie shrugged. "Remember how no one could describe the Big Blanket? The GETs' world and our world must be very different. To our senses, they seem invisible; our eyes reject them. Maybe they have trouble seeing us too."

"That's freaky," I said.

Elodie maybe noticed how worried I looked. "Hey, chill, eh? Maybe the GETs are harmless, like Little G. Space tourists or something."

I seized the thought hopefully. Alien space tourists, taking pics of the funny-looking human creatures just as we might photograph animals in a safari park. That was better than being invaded by killer monsters here to conquer Earth. "You really think so?"

"It's a poss. Mum thinks the Yellow Downpour could be space-fuel spillage. And the Big Blanket in Luxembourg could be a piece of some weird alien equipment." She pointed down a side tunnel. "They're still running tests on it to find out."

I frowned. "The Big Blanket is *here*?"

"Of course. And a fair bit of the yellow stuff. Both being analysed, big time." Elodie stopped and frowned back at me. "Don't you get it, Tim? This is the nerve centre of the whole alien investigation. Every bit of evidence we've found, every expert who could be any use is right here – or soon will be – working as hard and as fast as possible to decode this smell message and get our own space-travel system up and running. It's called the hyper-beam."

"I heard Dad mention that once," I realised. "He knew about this weirdo stuff. He knew!"

"Well, anyways . . ." She stopped walking, pausing impressively beside a big red door. "Rather than just sit around, we're doing our bit to help. Welcome to . . . the Crèche!"

She opened the door.

A vast, blank-faced yellow robot loomed over me, blocking the way.

I yelled, ducking under its arm and running blindly inside the room – for all of about two metres. Then I caught a blur of dark skin and blue T-shirt and WHUMP, I was on the floor beside another boy.

"I dropped it!" the boy (or, yes, OK then, boy-genius, as I was soon to find out) shouted. He had a classically geeky voice, with maybe a hint of Aussie thrown in. "The fission chip! I dropped it!"

"Fish and chips?" I echoed stupidly.

"Nooooooooo!" yelled Elodie, falling on all fours and scanning the floor. "Ray, can you see it?"

I couldn't believe them. "There's a ma-hoosive robot in here and you're worried about—?"

"No one move!" Ray looked panic stricken as he waved his hands over the tiled floor. "No one move, no one move!"

IT WAS A STICKY MOMENT, THAT'S FOR SURE! BY THE WAY, DO YOU LIKE THE COOL TECHNOLOGY I DESIGNED THAT ALLOWS ME TO INTERRUPT YOUR BOOK IN THIS WAY? COOL!

HELLO! HELLO, IT'S ME, LITTLE G! HELLO! I CAN SMELL THE TONGUE! HELLO!

ARGH, NOT YOU TOO, LITTLE G! I'VE ONLY GOT ENOUGH MONEY FOR 32 PICTURES IN THIS BOOK.

NOW, IT'S NEARLY TIME FOR THE END OF THE CHAPTER – WILL EVERYONE JUST SHUT UP AND LET ME GET ON WITH IT??!

So, anyway . . .

The yellow robot wasn't listening to Ray's pleas for no movement. It swung round to face us. Then it toppled forward, reached out for us with huge, gripping fingers . . .

SEVENTEEN

"Look out!"

Suddenly, unexpectedly, I found myself in action hero mode.

I grabbed a long metal tube from the nearest desk and swung it like a bat at the robot's head. **CLANG!** The blow made my arms jangle right back to my sockets but the robot was sent staggering! **YES!**

"Noooooooooo!" yelled Elodie again. "You just hit Kimmy with my quantum-flux polariser!"

My heroic pride quickly shrivelled. "Kimmy?"

Ray was glaring at me with big dark eyes. "That's not a robot, whoever-you-are! It's a nine-year-old girl wearing stilts inside a super-advanced mechanical suit."

"Kimmy!" Elodie was back on her feet and reaching out to the robot which was now teetering on one leg. "Don't put your foot down, you'll squash the—"

CRUNCH!

That was the sound of a fission chip's doom. Kimmy's robot foot squashed it good and proper.

Then there was silence, save for the whirr of the computer banks lining the walls, and the hum of the fluorescent strips lighting the room, and the bubble of chemicals on the various lab benches that stood dotted about like strange grazing animals, and the zappety-zap of massive 3D printers as they made mysterious components for still-more-mysterious machines, and the low drone of the several TV screens hanging from the exposed rock ceiling. So, not really silence at all, then (but still, as descriptions go it was kind of evocative, wasn't it?).

In short, this was like no crèche I'd ever heard of. And the kids in it weren't kids. From the look and sound of things, they were all geniuses.

Ray clutched his head like he'd been kicked there. "**Ohhhh, BOTTOMS!** It took me ages to program that fission chip."

I licked my dry lips. "I'm sorry."

Elodie grabbed back the metal tube from my grip, fuming. "And are you sorry about the dent you put in my fifty-thousand-Canadian-dollar quantum flux polariser?"

I cringed. "I didn't know! I thought it was just a big metal stick. I thought we were being attacked by a killer robot."

"By ME?" The robot pulled off its head to reveal a short Japanese girl, with bunches. "This ain't no flippin' robot, Mr Dummyhead. It is TAMASSISS – a Transcending All Matter And Sustaining Survival In Space Suit! And it's totally my design, so hands off. Try to copy it and I'll sue your butt off. Your butt will owe me its entire, um, butt."

"Kimmy is obsessed by legal action," Ray explained.

"Careful what you tell him, Ray," warned Kimmy. "He could be a spy."

"I'm not a spy, and I'm not going to rip off your design!" I protested. "I don't even know what that robot thing does!"

"Oh, sure. You oh-so-conveniently don't happen to know what the TAMASSISS does." Kimmy folded her arms and looked all sassy at me (TAMA-sassy, probably). "Like, you're just a simple, ignorant kid, huh?"

"Uh, actually Kimmy, I think he is." Elodie sighed. "Well, everyone. Say hi to Tim, eh?"

No one said anything.

A w w w w w w w w w w w w k w a r r r r r r r r r r d.

Finally, Kimmy held up a hand and Ray grudgingly said, "Hey, man." Then he started to stare at me with those big eyes. "He's really not like us?"

Kimmy nodded, wonderingly. "He's . . . *normal!*"

"Normal? Me?" Weirdly, I felt suddenly emotional. My whole life, I'd wanted nothing more than to be thought of as normal. And now, in here of all places, after being kidnapped and flown to the top of the world and chased by aliens, I'd finally achieved that blissful non-achievement I'd longed for all this time: normality.

"My dad's the clever one, not me," I mumbled. "What is this TAMASSISS transcending-matter thing? In words a dimwit like me can understand."

Elodie helped Kimmy climb out of the suit, which

was clearly meant for a full-sized adult, not a slightly annoying child. "This thing is protective armour we hope will keep astronauts together when they're using the hyper-beam travel system."

Ray nodded. "We're not going to just sit around while our planet's in danger."

Kimmy took up the propaganda: "So the Big Suits – you know, the scary secret spook guys in charge – let us use high-tech supplies from the stockrooms to give this place a techno-makeover."

My eyebrows flew up. "How did you get them to let you do that?"

Ray smiled modestly. "I just built a small bomb with some parts Kimmy took from the stores, and threatened to blow up the Big Suits' virtual golf course if they didn't give in to our demands." He honked with laughter. "Blow it up! Ha ha ha." He produced an asthma inhaler and scooshed a couple of puffs into his mouth. "Whoa. Good times."

"But didn't they just threaten to hurt your parents if you didn't behave?" I asked.

"Nope," said Elodie. "Cos we warned them that if

they did, we would have to switch on the antigravity pads we'd hardwired into their planes, satellites and space probes, smashing them into the roof and causing billions of dollars' worth of damage."

"We're like flippin' GANGSTERS," said Kimmy, striking a weird pose I guessed was her idea of what a gangster did. "Only, science is our gun, and intelligence is our, um, other gun."

"And when the Big Suits saw the quality of our work, they caved in straight away and gave us what we wanted." Elodie grinned. "It's pretty good, having that power."

"It must be," I said, wishing for once that I was clever, that I had the power to impress like that too. "What did your parents say?"

Ray grinned. "Mum said, 'That was clever of you, dear. Now, pass me that strontium rod and insert it into the neo-chemical matrix.'" He suddenly burst out into honks of laughter, like this was the funniest thing ever. Kimmy and Elodie guffawed too. "Hahahahahah, strontium rods, ha ha ha ha ha . . ."

"It's all about the strontium rods with your mum,

isn't it?" Kimmy wiped tears of laughter from her eyes. "My dad was like, 'You let them see your antigrav systems? You want them to steal your designs? What are you, flippin' NUTS? We could have sold them those designs for a fortune! If you have lost our family this fortune I will sue you for the full flippin' amount! And legal fees!'"

"Well, my mum was just relieved we used conventional explosives instead of radioactive materials," said Elodie, smiling. "She's very green, if you know what I mean. Obsesses over the environment."

Finally, something I could relate to. "I *do* know what you mean." I paused. "Although, I'm actually pretty glad you didn't make an atom bomb, too."

"Oh, we made one all right," said Ray casually. "We just decided not to deploy it."

"It's in the cupboard over there," said Kimmy.

"You've got, like, an atom bomb stored in your *cupboard*?" I stared at them. "Isn't that . . . dangerous?"

The others nodded solemnly. Then they burst out

laughing and high-fived each other.

"Your face!" Ray laughed so hard he needed another puff on his inhaler.

"We totally tricked you," said Kimmy, clutching her scrawny sides. "Of course we didn't build an atomic device." She grinned wickedly. "It's just an emergency bomb made using *conventional* explosives, in case we have to destroy our own work to stop the military stealing it."

"You can't be too careful, eh?" Elodie agreed.

"I hope you *will* be," I said out loud (while thinking "in quiet", *You're all completely bonkers!*).

"Anyway, the truly explosive news is that I think we're close to ironing out the bugs in this base's super-secret hyper-beam space travel system." Ray nodded eagerly. "El, did you calculate those matter-offset equations I asked you for?"

Elodie shook her head. "My mental maths took a nosedive thanks to Tim here. But it shouldn't take me more than a few hours." She rubbed her hands together. "I can't wait to see the looks on the Big Suits' faces when a bunch of kids solve their problems for them."

Kimmy nodded too. "It's gonna look SO sweet on my application to Cambridge University next year."

"Uh-huh, and when I sign up for my PhD at the University of California, Berkeley," said Elodie, also nodding. Everyone was nodding, except me. It was like they'd suddenly all turned into those weird toys with the wobbly heads. *Big* heads.

"Well, I'm sorry I messed up everything." I looked around the Crèche, trying to spot a spare place. "Um, is there anything *I* can do here?"

Ray considered. "Why don't you do some nice theoretical research in the work cubicle over there, Tim?"

"Probably because I don't know what you're talking about," I said.

Elodie shrugged. "OK, well, do you think you could maybe defrag the main computer's hard drive?"

"Defrag it? I didn't know it was fragged in the first place."

"Maybe you could just sit in the corner and draw a nice picture of a snowman," said Kimmy impatiently.

"No, thanks," I retorted, wittily. "I think maybe I'll just go back to my room and wait for Dad to finish. Back home, he was studying space-travel stuff – had me staying up all night timing bursts of ultra-cyclic radiation or something."

"Mmm, interesting," said Ray, although frankly I could think of nothing more boring. "What's your dad's name, anyway?"

"Eric Gooseheart," I said. "He used to work at the Strategic Space Centre—"

"No!" Elodie jumped back from me as if I'd burst into flame. "No way!"

I frowned. "He *did* work there."

"Get out. Stop it. No! No way. But then . . ." Elodie looked to have gone into a state of shock. "No. Nuh-uh. Enough of that. Quit it. He can't be. YOU can't be. Shut UP! I gotta . . ." She backed away, bumped into a lab bench and knocked her quantum flux polariser to the floor, where it sparked and went PHUT! She didn't even blink.

"Elodie!" Ray groaned. "Look what you did! Look!"

But Elodie wasn't looking at anything. She went

racing out of the Crèche like she had bats biting her bum. I watched her go, and all I could think of was . . . This girl talks about giant sense-shattering aliens, and the end of the world, like it's nothing. But when she hears who my dad is . . . *then* she freaks out?

Kimmy had scooped up the quantum stick-thing. "NOOO! Elodie bust the inner couplings." She shook her head furiously. "I should sue her!"

"You can't sue her, Kimmy," said Ray wearily. "You're only nine years old."

"That's defamation of character, Ray. I'm suing you too!"

"But you ARE nine!"

"Only in a numerical sense . . ."

Leaving them to it, I turned and walked away, my head awash with all I'd learned and seen.

Sergeant Katzburger was standing in the corridor, her Mohawk high, her wide face set in its usual hangdog expression. "Didn't go so well at Crèche, then?"

"Nope. "

"I knew it wouldn't." She sighed. "What did you say

to send Miss Uptight-Buns sprinting off like that? Never seen her move so fast."

"I have no idea." I sighed. "Actually, I have no idea about anything."

"Join the club, kid," said Sergeant Katzburger. "It's a lousy club. Its prices are kept artificially high, they play bad music and they never clean the washrooms. The club stinks. But you end up joining it anyway. That's life, kid. Or it is round here for dummies like us, anyway." She shook her head, miserably. "Wanna go to your room now?"

"I think I want to go to a whole other planet," I said.

EIGHTEEN

"Hey, I forgot to say." As we neared my room, Sergeant Katzburger brightened a fraction – which is to say, she only looked colossally glum instead of hideously depressed. "You're going to have a reunion."

Unaccustomed to good news of any sort, I looked at her oddly. "I am?"

"Sure," she said, "we got—"

"Little G! Hello!" came a familiar, jaunty growl beside me.

I jumped – but not very far, because two long green arms were wrapped around my waist.

"Hug, spaceboy!" Little G was gazing up at me. "It's you! Hug! I got the tongue . . ."

"Get lost, alien freak!" snarled Katzburger.

Little G scowled and held up his scrawny fists

and skinny arms like he wanted a fight. "Sargey Katzbonker make me? Huh? Huh?"

She pointed her gun at him. "You've got till the count of five to withdraw from this area, squirt."

"Uh-oh!" Little G squealed with terror and waddled off at high speed, sandals slapping down the corridor. "See you later, spaceboy! See you! Bye!"

Katzburger lowered the gun. "They should keep that thing locked up. He gives me the creeps."

"Better than giving you the hugs," I said shakily. I was glad he'd gone, but couldn't help feeling kind of sorry for Little G – used and abused and shunned by others. I could relate to that. *Typical, isn't it? I* thought. *I make a better impression on an alien from another world than on kids from my own.*

Katzburger grunted. "Anyway. What I was going to say is . . . your goldfish is here."

"Herbert?" I threw open my bedroom door – and there was my special fishy friend at last, darting about in his bowl, which now stood on the desk with a tube of fish food beside it. "Herbert!" I yelled happily and, as so often, I wished I knew what he was thinking now that he'd seen me again.

Herbert didn't look as bright orange as usual, but that happens to goldfish when they've been kept in the dark for a bit. I was so glad to see him and watched, delighted, as Herbert turned figures of eight in the water, thinking he must be pleased to see me, thinking how wonderful it was to be reunited with my pet . . .

For all of three joyful seconds.

"Did you know the collective noun for goldfish is a 'troubling'?" Katzburger piped up. "A troubling of goldfish. Yeah, well. They're troubling all right. Troubling to the soul."

Uh-oh, I thought. "They are?"

"I had my own goldfish, once, back when I lived with my folks in Minnesota. Six of them. Goldfish I mean. Six magnificent creatures of the deep."

A tank can't be very deep, I thought. But Katzburger's face had become a somewhat *less* magnificent creature of the deep*ly depressed*. She stared into the middle distance like people do on TV when they're having flashbacks.

"The boy next door . . . He threw a football and it smashed our window and knocked my hairdryer into the fish tank and my fish somehow turned on the hairdryer and the whole tank exploded in an unholy firestorm . . ."

If Herbert came with ears, I'd have tried to cover them. "That actually happened to you?"

"I was thirteen," she revealed. "And guess what? The boy only made such a lousy pass cuz he was distracted by weird lights in the sky."

"Wow," I breathed. "Is that what's made you sad all the time?"

"Partly," Katzburger admitted. "I'm also sad all the time because when I was fourteen, my pet dog was run over by a combine harvester. Guess what? The driver had been distracted by an unidentified flying object in the sky. And when I was fifteen, my tortoise was flattened by a falling piano — because the guys lowering it out of an upper storey window were—"

"Distracted by UFOs?" I surmised.

Katzburger nodded. "I went on to lose a mouse, a guinea pig, two hamsters and a boa constrictor thanks to idiots getting distracted by those lights in the sky. That's why I joined the military – so that one day I could join the secret anti-alien division and get some payback." She smacked her fist into her palm. "Justice."

"Um . . . is that why you don't like Little G?"

"If I didn't know for certain that the little alien squirt was a military prisoner during the years my pets were massacred – so he *couldn't* have been flying UFOs at the time – I'd have dealt with him, believe me." Her clenched knuckles were growing whiter. "No, I reckon these invisible GETs are responsible. And believe me, I'm gonna do all I can to make sure they pay for it. They will pay big time. Believe me. Oh, yes, they will suffer just as I have. BELIEVE ME."

I did believe her.

"Meantime, treasure your fish, kid," said Katzburger. "Love him. Be there for him. Let him help you try to make some sense out of this harsh, terrible life." She stomped away and slammed the door behind her.

"This place is full of nuts, Herbert," I confided. "But at least we have each other now."

Herbert drifted down to the bottom of his tank. Goldfish have no eyelids, so I couldn't be sure, but either Sergeant Katzburger's moaning had stunned him unconscious . . . or he was asleep.

It sounded like a good plan to me, too. So I made sure the door was locked, curled up on the hard little bed and fell asleep myself.

After dark dreams stuffed with exploding pets and hostile aliens, I woke up to the sound of knocks on the door.

"Who is it?" I called nervously.

"Dad," said Dad (factually accurate as ever).

I realised I'd been asleep for a whopping ten hours – and when I unlocked the door and saw how pale and tired Dad was, I realised guiltily he'd been in his meeting for just as long.

"Are they treating you all right?" Dad asked searchingly.

"Sure. Aside from the weird little alien who keeps saying 'hello' and trying to hug me and smell my tongue, and the hyper-smart gangster children in the Crèche, and the depressed soldier who wants revenge on aliens for accidentally causing the death of her pets, and . . ."

I began to dump my troubled, befuddled thoughts onto Dad, but it was my talk of Little G that took his real interest.

"All this stuff I've heard so much about, and seen on secret videos, and in conference calls, all of that . . . Here I can touch it! Be a part of it!" Dad actually smiled, gazing into space – in his head, *outer* space. "They've made so many strides forward with the hyper-beam, Tim! The actual projection of matter through the void . . . bypassing conventional rockets completely . . . We're so tantalisingly close to making green, environmentally friendly space travel a reality. But the system doesn't quite work." He scowled. "Little G must come from a race of geniuses – how come he's so stupid? It's not fair! We NEED him to make it work . . ."

"We can't all be super-clever," I said with feeling.

"The high-ups running this place think that Little

G is only *pretending* to be dim," said Dad. "They let him roam where he likes, but secretly he's being recorded at all times – in the hope he'll accidentally drop his stupid act one day and give himself away." He shook his head. "Apparently, he gets on best with children. He's more likely to drop his guard around you than with any of the adults who've held him prisoner."

I looked at him suspiciously. "Is that another reason why these Big Suits brought me and the other kids in the Crèche along? To get the truth out of a weird little alien?"

"I suspect so," said Dad. "They're desperate, Tim. Clutching at straws. They really feel that our planet is in mega-trouble, and we have to find the answer to the riddle of the space-projection system – urgently."

I felt my stomach churn. "Well . . . maybe Elodie and the others will come up with something. They're on the case."

"Elodie?"

"One of the kids I told you about."

"Elodie who?"

"Something weird. Um . . . Hongananner."

"HONGANANNER?!" Dad bounced off the little bed like his butt was full of springs. "You mean . . . she is the daughter of Hannah-Anna Hongananner?"

I nodded, startled. "How many Hongananners can there be in the world?"

"Too many," said Dad, pacing the floor like he was stamping on invisible ants. "Too many and too close and **NOOOOOOOOOOOO**, I can't deal with this now!"

I had never seen Dad so agitated. "What is it, Dad? Elodie freaked when I told her who you were, and now you're freaking when—"

"You told her my identity?" he hissed, red-faced with anger.

I shrank back. "Yeah! She asked me who my dad was, and I told her. What was I meant to say – it's Herbert?"

Dad buried his face in his hands and let out a soft, pitiful moan. "I should've known this would happen.

It was inevitable, I suppose." He walked to the door. "Well . . . I'm tired. Goodnight, Tim. See you in the morning."

I checked my watch. "Dad, it IS morning. It's half-past ten!"

He groaned again, and left. He slammed my door. I heard him open his own door. He slammed that one too.

Fantastic, I thought. *It's the end of the world, and Dad's cracking up.*

NINETEEN

Dad's snores shuddered through the wall. I just lay on the bed, chatting to Herbert – a pretty one-sided conversation as you can imagine. He kept bonking his nose against the glass as if trying to get out.

"I wouldn't bother, Herb," I told him. "Believe me, there's nowhere to go. Unless the aliens vaporise this entire base. Then the snow and ice will melt and flood the ruins, and maybe you can swim for it."

I wanted Dad to wake up so I could ask him why he'd acted so weird. Not that he'd ever agree to tell me. Like he'd never told me where I came from . . .

It's the grown-up's job to worry about their kid's behaviour, isn't it?

I thought back to Elodie's outburst. She clearly knew something about my dad . . .

Suddenly I heard a clanking noise in the ceiling

above me. Hot water pipes, I supposed. The ones in the Rubbish House had hissed and gurgled all the time. Stupid pipes. I felt a pang of homesickness for our old house in the city, and Nanny Helen. I wanted to see her now more than anything. If only she still lived with us, *she* could've been shot with a tranquilliser dart, abducted by scary men and dragged here with me, which would have been much better. Well, for me, at least.

THIS DIDN'T HAPPEN

One of the large ceiling tiles above me rattled. I looked up and frowned.

CRRAASH! The tile came hurtling down from the ceiling. As it fell, I glimpsed something lumpy and green riding it like a surfboard. THUMP – it landed right on top of me and whumped the air from my lungs.

"Hello!" Little G's big ugly face was suddenly in my own. "Hello, spaceboy! Hello!"

"UGHH!" I pushed him away, rolled out of bed and landed heavily on the floor, staring at him in fascination and revulsion. He'd changed his clothes, now wearing a skinny-fit superhero T-shirt, flip-flops and a kilt. "What the hell are you doing, coming through the roof?"

"Hello!" Little G smoothed out his top and straightened his medallion. "I heard you."

"But I didn't say anything!"

"You did." He looked at me, all three eyes intent. "Said you are home-sock."

"Home-sock?" I echoed.

Little G nodded. "You are sad. You miss your banana, mmm?"

"Homesick, you mean . . ." I stared at him, in wonder. "And it's my old nanny, not a nana. But I never said that out loud."

"You did, spaceboy!" Little G retorted. "Nana! Home-sock! You did just now!"

"But that was *after* you said you heard it." I was getting confused. "So how did you know?"

He opened his arms. "Hug? You want a big hug, home-sock spaceboy?"

"I'm not home-sock!" I insisted. "Homesick, I mean. Now, please, get out of here!"

"Wait." But now Little G was looking past me – at Herbert. "Hello!" He started bouncing on the bed excitedly and waving. "Hello! Hello!"

"That's my pet goldfish," I said. "He can't talk."

"Hello! Little G. Hello!" He hopped off the bed and came running at Herbert, his stumpy legs a blur. Instinctively I put myself in front of the bowl and held out my arms to protect it. But that seemed to give Little G the wrong idea.

"HUUUUG!" he warbled, jumping into my outstretched arms. "I smell the tongue! Mmm, tongue! Gimme, gimme!"

"Stop it with the tongue thing!"

"TONGUE!" Little G was wriggling like a big slimy puppy in tweed and sandals. **"Little G, TONGUE, spaceboy! Mmmm!"**

I was about to yell for help when the door swung open – and in stomped Sergeant Katzburger, her gun at the ready. "Step away from the goldfish!"

"Please, Sargey Katzbonker!" Little G whimpered. "Me need to listen to the tongue." He pointed to Herbert. "Put him in my mouth! Help you, spaceboy! You need help!"

"That's enough!" boomed Katzburger. She grabbed Little G by the back of his t-shirt and heaved him into the air. "No innocent pet fish is gonna get eaten by an alien! Not on my watch! Not ever!" She hauled the struggling Little G to the door and threw him outside where he landed with a **SPLUMP**. "And stay out of the ventilator shafts, too, or else! What do you think this is, a science-fiction film or something? Stay away from here. You get me?"

"Hug, Sargey Katzbonker?" called Little G pathetically.

"I'd sooner hug a nuclear warhead!" Katzburger slammed the door. "What *is* that thing's problem?"

"I don't know." I shuddered. "Thanks for the rescue."

"We have him under observation. When the monitors picked him up in here, I came running. Well, jogging. Well . . ." Katzburger thought some more. "I came striding quite quickly, anyway. Ish."

"I can't believe Little G!" I shuddered, though Herbert seemed unaffected, still bonking his head against the glass. "He scared the heck out of me, coming through the ceiling like that. What if he does it again and gets Herbert when I'm out?"

"I'd guard your fish myself, if I could." She sighed. "But I've got . . . other duties. Looks like I'm not going to be around here much longer."

"Really?" I felt a twinge of regret – Katzburger was hardly (Nanny) Helen, but at least I felt she was sort of on my side. "Are you being transferred or something?"

"Ha! You could say that. This is one heck of a transfer." She shook her head and her Mohawk quivered. "Well, before I go, I'll get maintenance to fix this hole. And I'll get security to bar the little green bonehead from entering the vents. That might help to keep your fish alive when I've gone. *Might*. But it may not." She paused. "In fact, it probably won't. Truthfully, kid, if your fish is marked for death by the cold momentum of implacable fate, well, that's it – he's gonna die. You can't stop that. I can't stop that. No one can. Death, death, death. It's inevitable. Death. For you, for me, for the whole wide stinking world. **DEATH**."

Well, that put a bit of a downer on things, as you can imagine. *Thanks for the pep talk,* I thought.

"I heard something top secret today," said Katzburger shiftily. "Wanna hear?"

I grimaced. "If it's top secret, are you meant to be telling me?"

"Nope," she said. "But what does it matter? Nothing matters. Nothing in the whole, wide, stinking world—"

"Please tell me," I said, hoping to dodge another lengthy road trip into misery.

Katzburger sighed. "You know that team of experts

trying to see past the Giant Extra-Terrestrials' invisibility shield thing? Well, they're getting somewhere."

"They are?"

"You saw the footprints on your way here, right?" She waited for me to nod, then went on. "Well, our special spy satellites have picked up similar footprints at the South Pole and in two other places – in the Borneo rainforest, and on one of the Galapagos Islands. And the team's come up with some special filters that show some kind of structure . . ."

"A structure?" I frowned. "So, they're building something?"

"No one knows what it is. But it's not gonna be good, is it? It's gonna be **BAAAD**. End-of-the-world kind of bad." She shrugged her shoulders and walked away. "Well, that's it. So long, kid."

Yeah, thanks, I thought. *After all her moaning, you'd think she'd be glad to be ditching the base for somewhere different. I know I would be.*

Once she'd gone, and it was just me and Herbert in my room again, I began to feel anxious at the thought of these giant alien buildings . . . Where were the Galapagos Islands, anyway? Where was Borneo? Wasn't that a type of dog chew or something? I needed to know . . .

There was a map in the Crèche. I could check it out, and check in with Elodie.

I waved bye to Herbert, left the room, locked the door behind me and set off for the Crèche, ready to tell the other kids my secret news . . .

Completely unaware of the secret news they were going to tell *me*.

TWENTY

When I went inside the Crèche, Kimmy, Ray and Elodie were working on new versions of the important parts that I'd managed to break the day before. And in the quiet booth in the corner of the room, reading a comic upside down was . . .

"Hello!" Little G jumped up when he saw me. "Hello! Hello!"

"What's he doing here?" I demanded.

Ray and Kimmy looked over, while Elodie remained apparently engrossed in her work.

"He was upset after he got thrown out of your room," said Ray. "He came here for some quiet time. You can see he's upset."

Little G was jumping up and down excitedly. "Hello, spaceboy! Hello!"

"He doesn't look upset," I argued.

"It was emotional cruelty, Tim!" Kimmy added. "That's pretty serious. Little G could sue you for that."

"He can't sue anyone, he's an alien!" I protested. "Besides, I could sue Little G for attacking my goldfish!"

"The tongue!" Little G crooned. "Come to papa!"

"Leave my goldfish alone!" I cried.

"Enough, already!" snapped Elodie. "People trying to work here."

Little G sighed and muttered a last, mutinous "Hello" under his breath.

"You have a goldfish?" Ray asked.

"Yeah, he was kidnapped with me and DAD." I emphasised the word, hoping for some further reaction from Elodie. "DAD got him for me when I was small. I've had Herbert my whole life thanks to DAD."

She kept on working and didn't react.

"Little G does seem very interested in goldfish," said Ray thoughtfully. "He likes watching all the crazy goldfish movies on YouTube."

"What crazy movies?" I wondered.

"Mmmm!" Little G grabbed a laptop in his long green fingers and flipped it open as he ran over. "Tonnnnngue! Look! Here! Hello!"

I saw several pages had been opened, with a different little film on each one showing goldfish turning loop the loops and wiggling about upside down, the kinds of trick that Herbert had learned to do.

"So it's not just *my* goldfish," I breathed.

"In me!" Little G patted his tummy through his waistcoat. "Mmmm! Nice tongue. Hello!"

"You are NOT eating my goldfish," I told him.

"G, could you go back to the quiet place?" Elodie called over without looking up. "Trying to work here."

I closed the laptop and handed it back to him. With a sigh, Little G waddled off back to the quiet booth. I supposed that at least while he was here I could be sure he wasn't chowing down on raw Herbert.

"So, Elodie," I tried again, "how're things?"

"Good, thanks." She looked up at me coolly. "You just caught me by surprise last night."

I waited for more, but it wasn't forthcoming. So I went on casually, "Weirdly, my dad reacted kind of similar when I told him about you."

"Did he?" Elodie jumped up, swaying like a beanpole in a high wind. "He grew emotional, eh? In a good way? Was he happy? Was he sad? Oh my god he was sad, wasn't he? Was he angry?"

Before I could speak, Kimmy jumped in. "Elodie!" she said sternly. "What have we agreed about displaying strong emotions in the Crèche during flippin' work hours?"

"Sorry, Elodie, but Kimmy's right," Ray joined in. "We don't have much time, remember?"

"Hug," piped up Little G, holding out his arms.

"Give me five minutes, guys." Elodie duly went over to the quiet booth and stooped to put her arms around Little G.

"Mmmmm," rumbled the weird little alien. "Hug!"

I looked at Ray. "You're right – there *isn't* much time. I heard something last night . . ."

"Uh-huh," he said knowingly, "about the hyper-beam system being a pile of pants that kills anyone who uses it, yeah?"

I froze, all else forgotten. *"What?"*

"Oh," said Kimmy. "Guess you *didn't* hear that."

"Hello!" called Little G, jumping away from Elodie. "Hello!"

"Shh," said Ray.

"What d'you mean, it kills people?" I asked, incredulous.

"Sure you can handle the truth, Tim?" Elodie said softly. "They say pets are often like their owners . . . and a goldfish has no stomach."

"True," I countered, sticking out my jaw. "But it *does* have a digestive tract about twice the length of its own body – and that's a lot of guts."

"Good for you, dude." Ray picked up a remote and one of the screens changed to show a view of a large, bright yellow room, empty except for a black circle on the floor and something like a massive electronic funnel hanging down from above. "The Big Suits here don't know that Elodie's hacked into their top-secret camera feed." He took a scoosh on his inhaler and started to rewind the footage.

"They've really been pushing the hyper-beam experiments lately," said Kimmy. "We think they're expecting some sort of showdown in space with the GETs . . ."

I felt a familiar tingle down my spine. Such incredible, far-out stuff, being talked about as though it were double Maths on a Tuesday!

"Trouble is, the Big Suits are dang-fast running out of volunteers for the hyper-beam project," said Kimmy. "It's probably a good job the astronauts *do* keep coming back dead and in pieces, or this place would be getting sued, like, a thousand times over."

I grimaced. "But . . . didn't they, like, test it out on dummies first?"

"Sure they did," said Elodie. "Plenty of dummies volunteered. Unfortunately, the hyper-beam turned those volunteers into vol-au-vents."

Ray pointed at the screen. "Here's a transfer they tried out last week . . ."

I saw a man in a hazard suit and space helmet, like

the one who'd turned up in the Rubbish House, walk into the yellow room and stand in the middle of the black circle. A red light flashed out from the funnel-thing, making the screen turn orangey. I braced myself.

"The idea of the hyper-beam seems to be this," said Elodie. "First, the projection unit shrinks you to the size of an atom. Then the travel beam opens up a tiny hole in hyperspace, draws you inside and spits you out at the place of your choosing, back at normal size. Then it's supposed to do the same thing in reverse to bring you back here. I say 'supposed to' because, so far, no one has actually *been* brought back . . ."

Suddenly the man on the screen vanished. The red light switched off. Ray fast-forwarded a bit.

"What's going to happen?" I asked gingerly.

"Brace yourself," said Kimmy. "Your eyes might sue the rest of your body for making them see this . . ."

I saw the yellow room on the screen darken suddenly as an unlikely shape appeared. It was a space boot. A space boot as big as a sofa, and gently steaming.

"That's what I call flippin' incredible *footage*," said Kimmy solemnly.

"It's all that's left of the astronaut after he's made the return trip," murmured Elodie.

"Humans get boot," said Little G quietly. "Boot. Hello! Boot."

"The astronaut's right foot?" I stared. "But . . . it's so big."

"Must be a mix-up in the matter-offset equations," said Ray. "To be fair, the fact that they got back any part of him at all is a positive. The hyper-beam normally loses them completely. Apart from the exploding guy. That wasn't good. He exploded."

I shivered and turned away. "Maybe they should just give up."

"They can't. Getting out there is too important, Tim." Kimmy took the remote from Ray and pressed some buttons. "Elodie showed me how to hack into the observation team's deep cosmic scanners too. Want to know what's out there in space between Mars and Jupiter? Do ya? Huh?"

"Don't forget to switch on the observation team's counter-alien eyesight filter." Ray flicked a switch. "There."

I saw a strange, blurred *something* on one of the other screens. At first my eyes didn't know what to make of it. It was a shimmering, solid, metallic but kind-of-watery square oval shape. And yes, I know that doesn't make any sense – despite the filter it was hard to make anything out. Even so, the more I stared, the more I felt a deep, primal fear flood through my lower intestine (cast-iron proof that, like Herbert, I really *did* have guts).

"That's the GETs' spaceship, isn't it?" I whispered.

"Yep," said Elodie softly. "That's it head on, pointed our way. Estimated to be thirty thousand miles wide, fifty thousand miles high, and maybe fifty million miles away."

Kimmy nodded. "And the Big Suits think that with technology as big and advanced as that, it probably has the offensive capability to fry all life on the planet."

I stared, as the invisible orchestra in my head launched into an ominous

DAA-
DAAAAH
DAHHHHHHHH!

Are you thinking what I'm thinking? Yep. This is a pretty good time to end a chapter.

TWENTY -ONE

I shuddered. "Let's switch off the picture."

"Don't lose sight of the obvious point here, Tim," said Ray, attempting a smile. "The aliens *haven't* fried us. That suggests they *must* be peaceful. Right?"

"What if they're planning something else," I said slowly. "Something . . . bigger?"

Everyone looked at me, ready to hear to what I had to say. Though I was scared to death, at the same time it was quite a cool moment.

So I told them what Sergeant Katzburger had told me about the aliens making . . . *something*. They listened in silence, and I crossed to the map on the wall to point out where the footprints had been found, together with the "structures" near the North Pole, at the South Pole, the Galapagos

Islands and Borneo.

And as I did so, I saw that the Galapagos and Borneo are both on the equator, on pretty much opposite sides.

The alien structures were sited at what you might call the four corners of the world. Not that they're really corners. But, well, you know.

"That's not just coincidence, is it?" I realised. "The GETs must have picked those places on purpose. They must have some kind of plan."

Elodie crossed coolly to a computer and started typing madly at the keyboard. "I am SO hacking into the observation team's Earth-scan database."

"Go for it," Ray told her.

"I've heard your mum talk about those four places, Ray," said Kimmy. "She and the other brainiacs working on the smell code reckon that the air is smelliest around each of those points on the globe."

"Uh-huh!" said Ray. "Conclusion: if the smell IS a code, then these structures have been set up to spread the 'message' – all over the world."

"Done it!" called Elodie, blowing on her fingers as if to cool them. "Hack attack complete! Here's Borneo . . ."

On the screen there was a blurry aerial view of some enormous, angular thing rising up from sprawling rainforest.

"It's some kind of machine," breathed Elodie. "Got to be as big as a skyscraper."

Kimmy switched the view to the South Pole. A similar shape stood there, glistening and shimmering amid heavy snowfall.

"Another one." I gulped. "Giant machines, pumping out stinky molecules."

"Sending out a message of some kind," Kimmy agreed, "and altering the atmosphere while they do it."

"Right," Elodie agreed, as the view changed to show a tropical scene, blighted like the others by the creepy blurred criss-cross structure. Finally, the screen showed the nearest structure, standing proud in the frozen Arctic landscape. I shivered to see huge, deep footsteps dotted around it.

"Wonder how long ago those were made," I muttered. The thought of one of these giant invisible monsters being so close made me want to run screaming to the nearest toilet.

"The new molecules in the air are still changing their pattern," Kimmy reported. "Maybe sometime soon when the change is complete, the GETs will act."

"And with a spaceship like that, they can destroy us, or invade us, or whatever-they-want to us!" I cried.

"Maybe today will be the day the hyper-beam starts working," said Kimmy brightly. "The Big Suits are planning another transfer today—"

"Transfer?" My insides seemed to choke. "Is that what you call the hyper-beam system jump thingies? Only . . . I think Sergeant Katzburger is next on the list."

Kimmy sucked in a breath sharply. "Katzburger?"

"Poor Sargey Katzbonker," sighed Little G. "Won't work. Hello! Trip never work with big ladies and big men. Tongue will tell! Please, spaceboy? Tongue?"

I was getting impatient. "Little G, which part of 'No Way' don't you understand?"

"Whoa!" Ray had brought some kind of flight schedule up on the screen. "Next transfer is scheduled for one o'clock this afternoon. The science team must think they've made another breakthrough."

"But if they haven't," I said, "whoever's in that beam will die!"

"We've got to work harder," said Ray, determination in every word. "I'm sure my fission chip can help create a stasis field around Katzburger before the system shrinks her."

Kimmy gave him two thumbs up. "And when my Transcending All Matter And Sustaining Survival In Space Suit is fitted with Elodie's quantum flux polariser it will make her intangible, able to pass through *anything* without harm. I'm *sure* that's a stage the grown-ups have overlooked." She scowled, gritting her teeth. "And if these military morons try to rip off my ideas for the TAMASSISS I'll sue their buns right out of their pants!"

"High five!" called Little G, both arms raised, looking lovingly at the four of us. "Group hug!"

"No!" we said in unison. Little G looked disappointed – then gazed past us to the door.

I will never forget what I saw there.

TWENTY
-TWO

I saw . . .

TWENTY -THREE

I saw a . . .

TWENTY -FOUR

I saw . . .

A tall, thin woman in a lab coat.

I know the fact that I saw an ordinary, tall, thin woman in the doorway is kind of an anticlimax after my big build-up. But think of it as a teasing mystery – *Why has Tim never forgotten Madame Tall-and-Thin, as she was not known to anyone?* Well, as you'll soon see, what happened next was all a bit . . . well . . .

"Dr Hongananner!" cried Kimmy.

"How do you do, ma'am?" asked Ray politely.

But Elodie did not look pleased. "Mum! I told you to stay away!"

"I couldn't, El." To my surprise, Dr Hongananner had an English accent, not a Canadian one. She was staring at me, tears in her eyes, and she was smiling and shaking her head. "Tim?" She said my name like it meant something in another language. "Tim . . ."

"Tim," Dr Hongananner continued shakily. "I just wanted to welcome you to the scary secret base thing, and . . . say hello . . ."

"Er . . ." I shrugged. "Hi."

"Hello!" said Little G brightly (and inevitably).

"Mum, I thought we discussed this?" Elodie looked grave. "I thought we'd agreed that saying something about *the situation* would only cause distractions and delay the big work and—"

"I'm sorry, El," said Dr Hongananner. "But events seem to be moving forward rather quickly and . . . I've heard something important and . . . I don't want to treat you like children . . . and though it's difficult to tell you, someone has to, and I . . ."

I felt familiar fear pinching at my stomach. "What's happened?"

"Well . . . now we've had time to study the work undertaken by, er, Tim's father, we think we've finally translated the first stink-code signals." Dr Hongananner smiled weakly. "Turns out there are actually two messages, released several weeks apart. And the really bad smell is different information again – we're close to cracking that too."

"Whoa, that's amazing!" declared Ray, like a polite schoolboy indulging his teacher. "I sure wish we were allowed to know what the messages say – but don't worry, we know you can't tell us."

Dr Hongananner sighed. "Don't give me that old chat, Ray. I know my daughter well enough to know she must be hacking into all the secret systems in this base."

"What?" said Kimmy, wide-eyed. "But even if she did, we would NEVER look at confidential information, I mean . . ." Then she sighed, dropped the little-girl act and growled, "Look, momma – don't even think of suing us, OK?"

"Shut up, Kimmy!" Ray hissed.

"It's all right. I just didn't want you to be alone when you broke into the encrypted files." Dr H pulled a printout from her pocket, gave us all a kind of seasick smile and started to read aloud as fast as a freight train. "The message says:

THE BIGGEST OF YOU TINY HUMAN THINGS MUST COME TO OUR SPACESHIP TO TALKY TALKY BIG LONG ABOUT HOW STUFF MUST TURN OUT NOW THIS IS AN IMPORTANT MEETING UNDER GALACTIC LAW STATUTE ALPHA-2-TABLE-5 AND INSTRUMENTS DETECT HYPER-BEAM THING AT YOUR NORTH POLE SO USE THIS AND COME TO OUR SPACESHIP

AT COORDINATES ONE-ZERO-SMELL-RED-FOUR-BLACK-ZERO SO YOU CAN HEAR OUR OFFER NOW WHY IS IT TAKING YOU SO LONG TINY HUMAN THINGS TO COME TO OUR SPACESHIP OUR LANGUAGE CODE IS SURELY EASY TO UNDERSTAND FOR ANYONE WHO HAS MASTERED HYPER-BEAM THING AND IF YOU DO NOT COME AND TALKY TALKY WE WILL ASSUME YOU DO NOT WISH TO TALKY TALKY AND WE WILL PROCEED IN OUR PLANS WITHOUT TALKY TALKY BUT DO NOT SAY WE DID NOT ASK YOU TO TALKY TALKY BECAUSE WE DID ASK YOU IN AN EASY-PEASY CODE ANY CHILD COULD CRACK AND YOUR NOT BEING HERE ON OUR SPACESHIP WHEN YOU HAVE HYPER-BEAM THING IS PROOF YOU COULD NOT BE BOTHERED TO TALKY TALKY AND PROOF THAT ALL LAZY TITCHY HUMAN THINGS ACCEPT THEIR INEVITABLE FATE WITHOUT PROTEST WHICH IS GOOD FOR US THE GALACTIC LAW CANNOT TOUCH US NOW THANK YOU AND WE WILL BE PROCEEDING WITH PLANS FOR THE PLANET NOW THANK YOU HUMAN THINGS BYE-BYE SLEEPY SLEEP.

The breathless burble of words expired. A long, dramatic silence followed. My blood felt chilled to crimson slush, freezing my whole body with its icy pulse.

"Uh-oh," said Little G.

Kimmy pushed out a long, low sigh. "Well . . . that is a serious bummer."

"Er, yes," said Dr Hongananner, stuffing the paper back in her pocket. "You could say so."

Elodie had turned pale. "Mum . . . is this game over?"

"Uh-oh," Little G said again. "Uh-oh, uh-oh."

"Uh-oh is right," I said quietly. "Cos we *haven't* mastered hyper-beam technology, have we? We took it from someone else, and we're still trying to make it work."

"But the GETs don't know that," Ray breathed. "They were waiting all that time for us to go talk to them about their 'plans for the planet'. But we never did, so they came down and built those . . . those . . ."

"Smell machines," Elodie suggested, "making sure their final message filled the air from pole to pole."

"But why?" I wondered. "What *is* this final message? What's it for?"

No one spoke. No one knew. But optimistic ideas like "Come visit our small chain of quality invisible-alien restaurants" seemed some way down the possible list.

"We HAVE to get the hyper-beam working!" Elodie cried. "So a space army can go up and meet the GETs and tell them to bug off!"

Ray's forehead was creased. "We've got to keep working on the problem. Maybe we can save Sergeant Katzburger and make the way safe for a whole space army to go out there and meet the GETs!"

"I suppose at least the work will keep your minds distracted," said Dr H. "But as for you, my poor Tim . . . I know you're not like these ones."

"It's OK," I assured her. "I expect panic and terror will keep my mind busy when the shock wears off."

"Ah. Shock. Yes. Speaking of shocks . . ." Dr Hongananner forced a serene smile onto her face. "Tim, would you care to join me outside in the corridor?"

"Great timing, Mum," growled Elodie. "I mean, we're only facing the probable end of the world and human civilisation, eh?"

"That's precisely why I *have* to say something!" her mum snapped.

"Just a bit on the late side!" Elodie turned away to a computer screen. "You drive me crazy."

Dr H looked downcast as she turned to go. "Come along, Tim."

I knew something big was coming. But what could be bigger than the news that aliens were planning a terrible fate for the world? How do you follow THAT?

It was hard enough just following Dr H outside – especially when Little G came after us. I waited for him to move on his way.

"Hello," he said, standing between the two of us.

"Er, this is a private matter," Dr H told him awkwardly. "So perhaps, if you wouldn't mind . . .?"

"Hello. Hello." Little G smiled, unwilling to shift.

"I guess he's not about to tell anyone," I said, keen to get this over with.

"Very well." Dr H smiled awkwardly and took a deep breath. "Tim . . . your father and I were married, once."

HUH? I stared at Dr H, and she stared back, as my world seemed to tilt.

"I'm not just Elodie's mum. I happen to be *your* mum too."

WHOA!

Shock shattered through every atom of my being as the words slowly sank in, numbing me like anaesthetic.

"I just thought I should mention it," she went on, "in case there isn't a chance to, later, because . . . the world's ended or something."

"HUGGGG!" cried Little G.

His joyful cry very nearly drowned out the orchestra in my head as they tried to start up the "Dah-dah-dahhhs" again. My legs turned to jelly. My head was threatening to follow. THIS . . . was my MUM? After all these years of being told I'd come from space, I was now actually LOOKING AT my mum! Or I *would've* been, if the world wasn't tilting all over the place. Mum-mum-mum-mum-mummmmm . . . It was all too much. Breathe! I couldn't remember how to breathe!

I heard her say, "Um, try not to stop breathing . . . er, son."

It was good motherly advice. But I was a rebel. You

can't just waltz into my life and tell me not to stop
breathing, Mother . . . !

And, wilfully, I fainted.

TWENTY -FIVE

I'd like to say that the mother I'd never known caught me as I fell. That would've been kind of sweet, wouldn't it? Well, apparently, she did try to catch me.

But she missed and I smacked my head on the tiled floor.

Dr Hongananner (or, Mum – MUM – **MUMMMM,** should I say? Should I? TOO WEIRD!) took me to the sick bay. Little G insisted on coming along too. Seems he didn't want to leave me. Sweet, huh?

There was a big queue for the doctor when I woke up, lying on three chairs pushed together. Since the alien message had been decoded, quite a few of the scientists had lost it and were running about the waiting room like loopers. Soldiers were trying to catch them – apart from those soldiers who were also running around like loopers. One of the *doctors* was trying to catch them. Little G had decided to join in the chase, waddling about and over the furniture in a discarded soldier's camouflage jacket – not because he wanted to catch anyone, I think, just because it looked like fun.

Fun. There was nothing fun about the way I was feeling. My head ached like a GET had stamped on it, but the thoughts of all I'd learned chased through my skull as clumsily as the poor hysterical loonies here in the waiting room.

"Huuug!" Little G yelled as a scientist stumbled into his sticky embrace. "Mmm, hug . . ."

Just then, just for once, I kind of wanted a hug myself.

I was staring blankly at all the running about, when suddenly Dad's tired and anxious face appeared right in front of me.

"Not talking," I said, shutting my eyes. "Go away."

"You *have* to talk to me," Dad insisted. "I've sent Dr Hongananner away. She should never have told you a thing like that."

"What, the truth about where I come from, you mean?"

"Yes! When Dr Hongananner broke up with me and left with my darling Elodie she promised never to come into our lives ever again and NEVER to try and contact you." Dad's left eyebrow was twitching, a sure sign he was becoming agitated. "And now Dr Hongananner has broken those rules, and I think it's . . . it's . . ."

"Did you call her Dr Hongananner all the time you were married to her, Dad?" I muttered. "That might have put her off a little. Is that why she left you?"

"You don't understand any of this, Tim."

"Because you never explain!" I looked at him, hoping the tears would keep out of my eyes. "So Elodie really is my sister?"

Dad closed his eyes and nodded. "Your twin sister, yes."

"Twin . . . ?" I shook my head – not only was the blabbermouth girl I'd only met the day before my sister, but we'd actually been roommates for nine months in the same stomach! "Why did they go, Dad?"

"I don't want to talk about it."

"Please."

"I think we should just forget it. No good can come from raking over old coals." He nodded assertively. "After all, coal is the number one contributor to climate change with the amount of CO_2 it releases—"

"WE'RE NOT TALKING ABOUT COAL!" I bellowed, ignoring the pain in my head. **"WE'RE TALKING ABOUT WHERE I COME FROM! THE PAST YOU'VE NEVER SHARED WITH ME BECAUSE YOU'RE TOO SCARED TO EVEN FACE IT!"**

The mad flapping about of the hysterical patients had been halted by my outburst. They all stood and stared at me, and were quickly caught and sedated by those who'd been chasing them. With the fun over, Little G came waddling up in a rush and got ready to throw his arms around me. But then he seemed to think better of it, and stopped.

"Hmm," he said, eyeing me and Dad. "Little G. Hmmm." Then he flip-flopped away, out of the waiting room.

"Thanks, son," called one of the doctors, waving a thumbs up. "Hey, Professor – you got a good kid, there."

Dad, beetroot red, said nothing.

"I guess I'm really *not* a good kid to you, am I, Dad? You probably would've preferred a robot." I narrowed my eyes at him. "There you are, the big genius, but when it comes to emotions you don't have a clue."

"I know all about emotions, thank you very much," Dad snapped. "Emotions pollute the mind! They're like bottles of dangerous chemicals – if you let them spill into your thoughts, they can cause a dangerous reaction."

"No reaction at all's pretty dangerous too, isn't it?" I glared at him. "Like, we didn't react to the aliens' message, did we? And now the whole *world*'s in trouble!"

Losing the last of my patience, I made to leave – but he took hold of my arm. "Wait, Tim. A full translation of the GETs' stink code is due to arrive any minute. I think we should face whatever lies ahead for the planet together – don't you?"

"N . . . O!" I spelled out to him. "You can face the end of the world but you can't face the fact that you used to have a wife – and I had a mum!"

With that I tore myself free of his grip and stormed out through the door and away down the tunnels. I had to find my room, but it wasn't easy with my head pounding and hot tears beginning to blur my vision.

On second thoughts – stuff my room! I wanted Nanny Helen here. I wanted her to be waiting the other side of the door with an "OMGeeeee!" and a huge hug. But she was a zillion miles away with another family now . . . Was this how Dad had felt when Dr Hongananner left him behind? I almost wished that Fist-Face Gilbert would suddenly appear, ready to take revenge; a punch would hurt but at least I understood that kind of pain – unlike the scary aching I felt inside . . .

Oh!!!

Still wrestling with my thoughts and feelings (and my underwear – I actually had a terrible wedgie), as I staggered towards a T-junction, I caught sight of a familiar figure in an oversized jacket, gasping and groaning as he waddled past ahead of me. A familiar figure accompanied by *another* familiar figure . . . It was Little G, using both skinny arms to help balance a fish bowl on his head.

As if I didn't have enough on my plate – Herbert was being fishnapped!

TWENTY -SIX

"Little G!" I yelled, rounding the corner and chasing after him. "Come back here!"

"Uh-oh!" Little G, struggling under the weight of the fish bowl, put on an extra spurt of speed. "Bye-bye. Bye-bye!"

I forced myself to run faster, but my head was killing me. "Stop running!"

"Can't, spaceboy! Can't!"

"You can! Just stop moving your feet!"

"I hear the tongue!"

"That's my fish!"

"Tongue! Tongue!"

I was starting to catch him up, when one of his rubber flip-flops flicked off the back of his foot and thwacked me in the face. SQUERCH! The slimy sandal stuck over my eyes, smelly and smothering.

"Ugh!" I groaned, tearing the foul flip-flop from my face; my eyes watered and stung with alien foot-juice, but I kept up the chase. I heard some beeps up ahead, like numbers pressed on a phone pad, followed by the CLUNK and HISSSS of a heavy door opening.

He's trying to hide in a side room, I realised. Without thinking, I followed Little G inside. "Honestly, G, if you hurt Herbert, I'll . . . I'll . . ."

A HISSSS and a CLUNK came from behind me. I realised the heavy door had slammed shut. It sounded how I imagined the door to a bank vault would close.

Wiping my eyes on my shirt, it took a few moments to work out where I was. And as I did, I felt my heart leap into my throat like it was trying to abandon ship.

I stood in a vast, bright yellow room, where a bulky figure in a spacesuit stood facing away from me in the middle of a black circle, waiting beneath a massive, metal techno-funnel that hung down from the black roof. A funnel that pulsed with a hundred

red lights and hummed with strange power.

I was in the hyper-beam room – and the figure was Sergeant Katzburger, getting ready to make her transfer into space.

"Hello!" Little G plonked down the fish bowl. The water sloshed about, but Herbert was still swooping inside, like a goldfish on an invisible rollercoaster ride. "Hello!"

"What are you playing at?" I stared around in panic. "We've got to get out of here!"

Little G nodded. "*You* got to get out of here!"

The hum of power was rising. There couldn't be much time left. I ran to the door, but there was no handle, only a keypad. "What's the code, G?"

"Don't know!" Little G chirped. "Sorry!"

He's an utter alien nutter, I realised grimly, turning back to the door. "Let me out!" I pounded on it, but it barely made a sound. Terror was squeezing my bowels from the inside. Where was that camera? I had to find the camera! I stared around, wild-eyed. Surely someone must have seen me on a TV screen somewhere in this place? Surely even now they were taking steps to abort the transfer, to get me and Herbert and Little G out . . .

Except, of course, half the staff were currently going crazy down at the medical wing. What if *no one* was watching? What if Ray and Kimmy were too busy working on their gadgets?

Katzburger still hadn't noticed a thing, standing in the circle as the power hum rose higher. I had to get her attention. Which meant running *into* the circle. The circle in which you stood waiting to explode, or to turn into a giant foot, or to vanish forever, never to be seen again . . .

What happened to you *outside* the circle? I didn't know what to do. I looked over at Little G to see what *he* was doing.

He was eating my goldfish.

"Mmm! Hello!" Little G dangled Herbert between finger and thumb, over his wide smiling mouth. "MMMM, I got the tongue! Hello! In you go!"

Then – *PLOP! GULP!* To my disbelieving horror . . . Herbert was swallowed whole.

"NOOOOOOOOOOOOO!"

I ran up to Katzburger, shock smashing at my senses yet again. "Please, Sergeant! Little G's gone bad! He's eating Herbert! **HE'S EATING MY FIIIIIIIIIISH!**"

But Katzburger had already seen what was going down – more accurately, what was going down Little G's throat. And quick as lightning she tore off her space helmet and burst into action. "No you don't, you little green punk!" she roared, lumbering forward. "No innocent pet is gonna die at alien hands on *my* watch!"

Little G turned and ran, arms waving high in the air, his borrowed camouflage jacket scraping the ground. But Katzburger was a woman on a mission. She charged up behind him, threw both arms around his chest and squeezed violently – once, twice – like people do to help someone with something stuck in their throat, trying to jolt it loose. I watched, transfixed, hoping against hope . . .

Then, over the fierce whine of the building power, Little G gave a kind of strangled, choking noise. Herbert flew out of his mouth like a surface-to-air missile, soaring through the air . . .

I started forward to try to catch him – but couldn't move from the big black circle.

Uh-oh. The hyper-beam was activating!

I saw Little G and Katzburger charge forward to catch my goldfish. "Be careful!" I yelled – or rather, I tried to. But now the hum had grown so loud it swamped everything, and the air about me felt too thick for words to penetrate. Everything was turning orange . . . more orange than Herbert himself. The haze fuzzed up further, till I could no longer see the struggling figures.

Transfer's underway, I realised. *I'm going . . . I'M GOING* . . . I had no spacesuit, no protection, no hope – and very probably no clean underwear. I started to pant like I was a deranged dog, and felt a sharp, painful buzzing through my body – like I was a massive mobile phone set to vibrate . . .

And then blackness rushed in. Not an "oh-look-I'm-unconscious" kind of blackness. This blackness was speckled bright with dots of light. And it was everywhere, stretching out around me as if floor and sky had turned into enormous IMAX cinema screens.

I wasn't in the hyper-beam room any longer. Transfer was complete. I was suspended in space.

Outer Space.

look over page

The situation was so vast, so incredible, I couldn't take it in. My poor, bruised, battered sanity almost fled my head screaming as I tried to take in the sheer scale of the universe about me.

The view was endless and pinsharp – blackness and brightness. A distant boulder caught the starlight as it tumbled serenely past. A ball of light, dazzling but way smaller than the sun, was . . . well, the sun – only further away. Could I be out somewhere near Mars?

Suddenly I was afraid – that vague thought of geography had given me some perspective. I'd started to think about my position. My hopeless, deathly position.

Tim Gooseheart, first boy in space. Without a spacesuit.

I was lost. A tiny, insignificant thing, no more than a grain of sand on a beach the size of infinity. This is why they call it space, I thought, dangling in the eerie, airless vacuum. There's so *much* space . . . stretching on endless and forever . . .

And it was cold. Freezing cold.

As panic rose, I pushed out my last breath. I tried to breathe in some more. I couldn't. No air! Duh! That's why it was an airless vacuum. I was suffocating!

My ears hurt, like they wanted to pop only a hundred times worse. Was I going to explode? My arms and legs were already tingling. My eyes were stinging. A terrible chill was spreading through me, but my tongue felt weirdly hot.

Little G called me spaceboy. Was he planning this whole thing all along?

I tried to turn, but it was difficult, floating gravity-free in the emptiness. I didn't know which way up I was. Then I saw it – a huge, extravagant blur of light behind me. A structure that shimmered and trembled, stretching up into the infinite like a cliff with no top. It could only be the GETs' spaceship.

I still couldn't breathe. Panic was shaking me. My ears were hurting more. I'd only been out here maybe ten seconds, and it felt like I was going to burst out of my skin. There was a metal taste in my mouth. My eyes were stinging worse. I felt the water on my tongue begin to bubble.

The last thing I saw was the weird, alien ship, pulsing, flickering . . .

Then my brain must've used up the last of the oxygen in my blood. There was no more to be had, and no time to think of any brave final thoughts, no breath to say bye to Dad and the mum and sister I'd barely met, or the fish I'd left behind with an alien goofball and the woman who should've perished here in my place . . .

I made like the rest of space – and blacked out.

TWENTY -SEVEN

I wasn't expecting to ever open my eyes again. But somehow, there I was, Tim the spaceboy, alive – ALIIIIIVEEEEEEEE, I tell you! – and in a different kind of darkness now. An *inside* darkness. Some kind of room.

They got me back! I thought. The hyper-beam worked after all!

I tried to move. Everything ached. My face felt sunburned, my eyes were sore and my tongue was numb, but otherwise I seemed OK.

But how long had I been gone? Where was I? Back in the base? The sick bay, maybe?

My surroundings were blurred and vast, stretching up into pulsing shadows the colour of dried blood. I rubbed my eyes. If I wasn't back at the base, the only other place I could be was on board the spaceship.

The GETs' super-massive ALIEN spaceship.
Yeah. That was a happy thought.

AAUUUGHHHHHHHHHHHHHHHHH!

My howl of anguish and terror echoed around the nightmarishly ma-hoosive dimensions of this strange, unknowable domain.

As it died away, I heard a scuttling sound. Something dark stirred in the crimson gloom – huge and crooked and twitching, like giant spider legs. The shadows shifted, and with a clacking, clattering noise, the thing was gone. I held absolutely still as whispering voices came hissing out of nowhere – more in my head than in my ears, if that makes any sense.

"Silence!"

"Be hushed at once! We have saved you!"

I shut up as they said. Best to be polite when you find yourself on board a sinister alien spacecraft belonging to Giant Extra-Terrestrial beings, millions of miles from your home.

"You saved me?" I breathed, still terrified.

"Yes. Your crude hyper-beam projected you only close by to the coordinates we supplied," came the sinister whisper. "Now, silence we say!"

"You are very late," said the second sinister whisper. "Your protection under galactic law has almost expired." There was a pause. "Shall we send the trigger pulse to the great machines as planned?"

"Yes," crowed Sinister Whisper One. "This ambassador's agreement is a certainty in any case."

"Er . . . What does 'send the trigger pulse to the great machines' mean?" I asked.

"You will know in time."

"And . . ." I gulped. "When you said 'ambassador', were you talking about *me*?"

Sinister Whisper Two came back to answer. "Who else . . . Mr President."

My heart banged like typewriter keys being whumped by a gorilla with anger issues. Mr President? Was *that* who they'd been expecting?

Of course it was. An ambassador – someone important who could represent his planet in talks with enormously powerful alien beings. The President of Planet Earth. And instead, who had they got? Tim Gooseheart, the most ordinary, average twelve-year-old boy in the world.

Have you ever felt out of your depth? Magnify that feeling one hundred squillion times . . . *two* hundred squillion times . . .

"Silence!" Whisper Two rasped suddenly. "Our business partners require full tranquillity. They must not be disturbed."

"But, I . . . I didn't say anything," I protested.

"Activate the emo-shield," Whisper One instructed.

"It should've been raised the moment we took this Earth thing on board."

I didn't like the sound of an emo-shield, but I kept quiet, my mind racing. I could hear the sinister whispers having a private chat, but only caught the odd word or phrase: "*Switch on . . . transformation of the air . . . prepare . . . silent world . . .*" The sound of scuttling in the blur of dark red shadows all around me was growing louder, I was sure.

"Please," I squeaked, "send me back. I shouldn't be here. There's been a mistake!"

"A mistake?" Whisper Two didn't sound impressed. "You are NOT entitled to speak and act for the human race?"

"Um . . ."

"No matter," said similarly unimpressed Whisper One. "The time for appeal has nearly lapsed in any case. We can give this human thing to the chittersnipes."

I didn't know what a chittersnipe was. I didn't want to find out.

"Wait! Uh . . . Sorry, of *course* I'm the President.

How do you do." If these whispery things were too alien to realise I was just a kid, I wasn't about to commit suicide after all I'd been through by telling them the truth. "We, uh, welcome you to our planet and . . ."

"YOUR planet?" Whisper One was growing louder, raspier, scarier. "This world is OURS! It has been in our family for two billion years . . ."

"It is our holiday home," Whisper Two added. "We had a lovely thousand-year vacation here, three hundred and fifty million Earth years ago. It was a peaceful world with only primitive plants, fish and insects under our feet. Imagine our horror when we returned to find creatures like YOU had evolved and multiplied and INFESTED the whole place!"

My stomach juices turned to lava and started bubbling. *Dad was right*, I realised. *Humans are like dung beetles. Our dungball belongs to bigger beetles and now they're taking it back.*

"We . . . we didn't know it was your planet," I said feebly. "Er . . . Sorry for evolving and stuff, but we're kind of living on it now."

"Wrecking it, you mean," Whisper Two said indignantly. "The atmosphere was a polluted mess. We had to get the decorators in."

"Decorators? So THAT's how all the pollution just disappeared?" My brain felt ready to break the boggle barrier. "You kind of . . . painted over it?"

"Well, we couldn't sell the planet in *that* condition, could we?" said waspish Whisper One.

"Let me get this straight," I murmured. "You're going to SELL the planet like it's just a house or something?"

"Yes," said still-sinister-overall-but-quite-chatty Whisper Two. "It was the cosmic rays in this part of space that used to make it so attractive – but they have dissipated now. And the planet is too far from the galactic trade routes to sell to a business. Happily, we *have* found buyers – a family from our sister race, the Ova-Many. And once the nursery is prepared—"

"Enough talk," Whisper One broke in.

I frowned. "Nursery?"

"The information is irrelevant to your future."

175

A long, long silence followed. And through the fog of my helplessness, a thought broke into daylight – how can I understand these GETs? I thought they only spoke in smells or whatever? Are they translating their smells? If so, they pong excellent English. In which case, why didn't they just transmit their weirdo message in a human language?

Didn't they *want* us to understand the message . . . ?

"Let us conclude this business properly." Whisper One wafted back in my ears. "There is something you must understand, Mr President . . ."

A strange smell tickled the back of my nose – a smell I had no words for. And then, I heard footsteps – someone approaching with a heavy, confident stride. A familiar figure stepped out from the shadows ahead of me – and my eyes almost exploded with shock.

"Y-y-y-y-y-YOU?"

TWENTY -EIGHT

Darren "Fist-Face" Gilbert.

There he was, standing just a metre away, looking scarier and meaner than ever I'd seen him.

HUH?!

Fist-Face. On a spaceship. In space. Dressed in his ragged school uniform.

"What you looking at, Goosefart?" he growled.

"That's *President* Goosefart to you," I should have replied. Or maybe, "Er? HELLO? I think I'm allowed to look a bit weirdly at you, Darren, seeing as you've just turned up out of nowhere on a Giant Extra-Terrestrial spaceship!"

But of course I was scared to death and could only manage to say: **"Errrrrrughhhhhhh . . ."**

Fist-Face pointed to a piece of old, yellowed paper on the floor in front of me. Where had that come from?

"Sign this," he snarled, "or I'll pummel you into juice."

I stared at the paper, unsure and unwilling to accept any of what was now happening. "Fist-Face," I managed at last, "how did you get here?"

"Don't ask stupid questions," he retorted.

Again, I should've said, "I think you'll find it's quite an intelligent question to be asking, actually, considering you're a fourteen-year-old homicidal maniac who can barely travel into school on the bus, let alone zip tens of millions of miles across space to threaten me with a pummelling." But a new smell now whistled about the back of my senses. A distracting scent . . .

Of course it made sense that Fist-Face should be here. And if I didn't sign the paper as he wanted, I would get pummelled into juice. Obviously, I didn't want to be pummelled into juice. *I MUST SIGN IT,* I thought.

But I hesitated.

"Sign the paper," said Fist-Face impatiently. "Or else."

"Or else what?"

"Or else . . ." A nasty smile spread over his already very nasty face. "Or else Nanny Helen will love her new family more than she ever loved you."

I could feel my face clouding over like a day at Wimbledon. "Huh? What would you know about . . . ?" A fresh scent skulked in my nostrils as the shadows shivered again. And suddenly, Nanny Helen was walking forward, just as she'd looked the last time she'd called round.

"OMGeeeeeeeeeeeeeee," she cried, standing beside Fist-Face. "My new family are SOOOO lovely! I think I will definitely love them all more than I ever loved you, Tim, just as you feared!" She looked at me with dark eyes. "Unless, of course, you sign that paper on the floor in front of you, Tim. Then I will love you best and be your nanny for always! OMG, isn't that cool?"

She sounded so reasonable. Not the words, so much – they sounded as ridiculous then as they do writing them down now – but something about the way she spoke was so reassuring.

I stooped and picked up the paper and tried to read what it said. It seemed blurry, hazy, flecked with half-formed shapes and colours. I looked at Nanny Helen, standing there with her arms outstretched ready to hug me. But as I walked forward to hug her back, she lowered her arms and shook her head.

"Not until you sign, Tim!" she said sadly.

"You wouldn't be like that," I muttered. "If you were real, you wouldn't act this way . . ."

Fresh smells. I was feeling sick.

"Well, I'm deffo real, Tim," said Elodie, walking out of the shadows behind Fist-Face. "You know I'm real, however much you wish I wasn't. And you also know that Dad's spent the last eleven years wishing Mum had taken *you* with her when she left instead of taking clever old me . . ."

"No," I breathed.

"Dad's always been disappointed with you," Elodie persisted. "He thinks you're stupid and rubbish and a waste of time."

"That's not true!"

"It *is* true, brother of mine," said Elodie, and both

180

Fist-Face and Nanny Helen nodded. "Unless you sign the paper of course, eh? Then it won't be true at all."

"Huh?" I shook my head, trying to clear it. There were so many fumes in my nostrils: my nose felt like a factory's smokestack. "That doesn't even make sense."

"It does so too make sense," said Hannah-Anna Hongananner – MUM – coming into the hazy light. "Come on, Tim. It's just a piece of paper. Sign it and I will be the mother you never had. If you *don't* sign it I will hate you and call you names like 'plop-muncher' . . ."

"Stop it!" I tried to throw down the paper, but it seemed glued to my grip. "This is crazy."

"Sign the paper, Tim," said Dad, who had somehow appeared behind Fist-Face. "If you do, we can move back to our old house."

"How can we?" I sobbed, clutching my spinning head. "Someone else is living there now."

Dad smiled. "Removing people from their homes is easy."

"Sign the paper," said Fist-Face.

"Sign it," chanted Elodie and her mum – *our* mum – as Nanny Helen joined in. "Sign it! Sign it! OMG, sign it!"

"Sign it!" Little G's voice rose above the chorus. "Sign it! Hello! If you sign it I will un-eat your fish! Hello! Little G!"

The babble was overwhelming. The mingled stinks in my nose were mangling my senses. I fell to my knees. I couldn't bear it any longer. I needed this madness to stop. And all they needed me to do was sign . . .

There was something like a pen in my hand.

I put the paper back on the floor.

I scribbled down my name.

The smell in my nostrils suddenly vanished. Fist-Face vanished. Nanny Helen vanished. Little G, Dad, Elodie, Mum (**MUM**!!!) vanished.

"They weren't real," I realised shakily. "It was all . . . in my head . . ."

"Yes, Mr President," said Sinister Whisper One. "An illusion, created by us. We knew you couldn't resist your deepest fears. Now, let the chittersnipes retrieve the document . . ."

At the sound of the voice, the dark, hard, spidery thing I'd glimpsed before scuttled out of the shadows. And there were more behind it. Lots more. Unlike the GETs, these were solid monsters you could see, each as big as an armchair, carried on spidery, stick-like legs. Dark blue hands, tons of them and all shapes and sizes, stuck out from the lumpy bodies, clutching and questing. And wherever an arm *didn't* grow, a tusk-crammed mouth opened instead . . .

Sinister Whisper One came back for a parting shot. "We're obliged to you, Mr President," it rasped. "Your signature makes everything nice and legal."

"You tricked me into signing it!" Terrified now, I stared down at the paper I'd signed. "What is this thing, anyway?"

"Just a little permission slip in case the galactic cops come sniffing around." There was no mistaking the whisper's smugness. "Now the sale is nice and legal, plans for the Ova-Many nursery can continue without delay. Chittersnipes – take the paper . . . and deal with the human thing."

Panic rose like seawater about my nervous wreck as the whispers turned to deep, throaty laughter – and the chittersnipes bundled forwards to get me.

TWENTY -NINE

The chittersnipes were moving towards me so fast, I was left with little more than a moment to stuff the piece of paper I'd signed down the back of my trousers in the hope these creatures would never find it – or that if they ate me, maybe they would eat the paper too and erase my terrible mistake.

That left me with a nanosecond to reflect that I was about to die in a really, really horrible way. There was a soundtrack to these thoughts, but it wasn't especially banging. It was just me screaming: **"NOOOOOOOOOOOOOOOO!"**

Until the drum of stamping footsteps cut through the clamour. I looked past the approaching chittersnipes to see . . .

Kimmy's yellow metal TAMASSISS – the Transcending All Matter And Sustaining Survival In Space Suit –

stomping towards me!

It's another illusion, I thought.

Then a yellow-clad arm snatched me up from the ground like I was no more than a Tim Gooseheart action figure (*He walks! He talks! He accidentally betrays the world while pretending to be its president!*) and yellow-clad legs whisked me away from the chittering chittersnipes.

"The emo-shield is breached!" Sinister Whisper Two was crackling with outrage. "Silence them! *Silence them!*"

The chittersnipes chased after us through the weird, warping darkness, all teeth, arms and legs and unearthly yowls.

"Kimmy!" I cried. "You saved me!"

"Saw the GETs take you on board on the deep-space scanner," came a deep voice from the suit.

"You're *not* Kimmy!" My relief started turning to despair with spectacular speed. "Who are you?"

"Later, OK?" came a deep, muffled voice. "OK?"

I couldn't put up much argument. And in fact, I didn't have time to worry about who was saving me, as a speckled yellow light engulfed us both, and we ran STRAIGHT THROUGH a shadowy wall . . .

And out into space.

Kimmy said the suit could pass through solid objects, I remembered, and that anything caught up in its energy field would travel with it. Once again I was left gazing at the terrible, pitiless enormity of the universe. Once again I couldn't breathe, couldn't speak, couldn't shout, **"YOU CRAZY MANIAC, WHY DID YOU SAVE ME FROM THE CHITTERSNIPES JUST TO KILL ME IN OUTER SPACE?"**

Then I thought – how *can* we be out in space? I thought the GETs' spaceship was thousands of miles long?

As the TAMASSISS powered on through the blackness, I twisted in its grip and suddenly saw that we were headed straight for *another* ship, hidden behind the first. It had to be the Ova-Many ship.

OVA-MANY SHIP

GET SHIP

NOT TO SCALE

It played games with my eyesight, towering, shimmering, barely there one moment and hard as glass the next. What if we didn't pass through it? What if we slammed right into it and exploded?

My body yanked up hard on the handbrake of fear.

The TAMASSISS finally glowed yellow again and we were inside – I could breathe again. The suit allowed us to pass through the hull of the Ova-Many ship, into shadows that were somehow softer, warmer.

The whispering GETs had said that the Ova-Many were a sister race; did that mean they were just as scary? I didn't want to find out – I wanted to *get* out.

Then a sound started up, or something *like* a sound. I didn't really hear it as such. I *felt* it: a hideous cacophony of shrieks and wails, a billion daggers of noise thrown at my senses to tear them apart.

"What is it?" I yelled, clutching my ears. "Burglar alarm?"

"No," said the TAMASSISS. It was still running with me, and another wall threatened. We glowed golden bright once again, and then . . .

Through. Our surroundings changed. The light

was pink. The space seemed infinite. The stink was dreadful, a stronger version of the alien stink back on Earth.

And the roaring tidal wave of noise seemed to build, a hundred times louder.

"This suit now incorporates the special see-anything visor, OK?" The TAMASSISS was still running relentlessly forward. "Share my view. OK!"

The gold prickles in the energy field around me grew greater. Trying desperately to cling to my reason, my eyes made sense of the scene around me.

It was as if we were running along a path at the bottom of some vast valley – except instead of steep hills, on either side there were gargantuan aliens: huge, skinny and grey, with oversized heads and faces like plasticine poked about by a bear with a headache. They were wriggling beneath giant blankets . . .

Like the Big Blanket down at the base, I thought, numbly. *The Big Blanket that dropped out of the sky and crushed Luxembourg.*

The whopping great creatures were kicking strange

limbs, squashed up beneath their blankets in their own individual metal trays; each construction was angled to the ground like a playground slide. It was hard to make out features, but the colossal pits quivering in each monstrous face looked like mouths. Wide-open, wailing mouths, screaming like . . .

Like babies, I thought. *This place is crammed full of hyper-humongous, Ova-Many BABIES swaddled in giant, huggy-sucky blankets!*

"OMG," I said, channelling Nanny Helen in my time of crisis. "The nursery those GETs were whispering about . . . it's meant for *these* things! No wonder they didn't want any noise disturbing the Ova-Many babies if they make THIS racket when they wake up!"

One of the monstrous babies screamed even louder – and a river of yellow filth burst from its mouth hole, like a million-dollar, oddly-coloured oil-strike erupting from a well.

With a thrill of horror, I remembered the Russian village destroyed by the Yellow Downpour. And now I knew it wasn't space fuel spillage like Elodie had suggested.

It was projectile alien baby-sick. And I was right in its steaming path.

"Keep running!" I yelled to the TAMASSISS, but it was no good – we were like tiny bugs in a bath running from the hot tap. Except if this flood touched us, we wouldn't just be swept down a plughole. We'd disintegrate or burst into flames or . . .

Suddenly, even as we ran, a red haze enveloped us. The whole spaceship seemed to be shaking. I heard rasping, hissing voices carry angrily over the din – the GETs still in pursuit, or the Ova-Many wanting a piece of us . . . ?

Then the TAMASSISS and I weren't there any more. We were back in the centre of the hyper-beam room running out of the black circle and—

KRANNG! Into the wall.

The TAMASSISS dropped me and collapsed. I fell with it to the floor – where I showered the tiles with little kisses, so grateful to be back in my own, ordinary world.

I felt something scratchy around my bum area. With a thrill, I realised it was the paper! I might have been tricked into signing whatever it was, but the GETs didn't have the evidence! YESSS!

Then I noticed a body. A big silvery form – someone in a spacesuit. They were lying slumped beside the heavy door, the space helmet removed to reveal the face of—

"Sergeant Katzburger!" I struggled up and staggered over to check she was OK. Her eyes were closed but she was still breathing.

Then I realised that Little G and Herbert were nowhere to be seen; Herbert's bowl stood empty, save for one of Little G's flip-flops floating in the water. With all I'd been through, I'd forgotten my poor little fish, eaten by the bonkers little alien. Where could they be? Surely they had to be somewhere . . .

"Sergeant Katzburger is sleeping. OK?" The TAMASSISS had recovered and was standing up, facing me across the room. "Everyone in the world now sleep. Except you."

"Huh?" I stared at the blank-faced yellow suit. "What did you say?"

"The adults finally translated the smell code," the

TAMMASSISS went on its deep, husky voice. "The GET stink-machines have transformed this planet's atmosphere into lullaby gas. Made all animals go to sleep!"

I groaned. *Our clients require full tranquillity*, the GET had said. *They must not be disturbed.* And then it had triggered the pulse thingy, to set the lullaby going. "Dad! My . . . *mum*. Everyone! **ASLEEP?!**"

"You and me, the only two awake in the whole world." The suit continued its lament: "The Ova-Many children raised here will be soothed by the lullaby. But no Earth land animal will ever reawaken from its spell . . . spaceboy."

I froze. "What did you call me?"

The TAMASSISS reached up and pulled off its yellow helmet . . .

To reveal the crazy face of Little G!

Except Little G was no longer little. He wriggled out of the heavy protective suit, taller than me now. His camouflage jacket was the only thing that fitted him, and his voice had grown bigger to match.

"Hello," he said, looking as serious as a big alien

with two noses, an ear in the middle of his face, three eyes and a camouflage jacket can get. "I am **BIG** G, OK? Guess what, spaceboy – it's us against the aliens!"

THIRTY

"*Big* G?" My mind throbbed like it was about to explode. I backed away until I came up against the door. "Us against the aliens? But . . . you ARE alien! And you've changed . . ."

"Different alien," Big G agreed. "Not like GETs or Ova-Many. Hello."

"Don't just hello me! We've got to do something! What if the GETs send their chittersnipes here to get us—?"

"They will most likely scan planet to find where we are."

"And the Ova-Many will be really mad at us!"

"True. We in massive trouble."

"Stop agreeing with me!" I was ready to tear my hair out. "I can't do anything. Nobody can – they're all asleep. We're doomed. The whole planet is doomed!"

"Don't say that, spaceboy," Big G chided.

"You mean . . . there's hope?"

"No, it's just so depressing!" Something of Big G's old, cheeky self showed in his sudden smile. "Listen. I am on your side. Can Big G hug big invisible aliens? NO WAY!"

"I guess you did save me back there . . . Thanks." I shook my head, utterly astounded. "You're so different now."

"I will try to explain." Big G pressed some buttons on the keypad beside the door, and the door hissed open. "But while we talk, we must send Kimmy, Ray and Elodie out into the airless vacuum of space."

"HUH!?"

"Just like happened to you," Big G went on quickly. "Hyper-beam will remove effect of stink particles from their bodies. You been breathing the lullaby air for months, just like everyone else, spaceboy. Now you are the only human in the world still awake cos hyper-beam took you apart and put you back together, scrambling the alien code in your blood. OK?"

As I tried to take this in, I saw base staff sprawled

and snoring in the corridor outside. "I'm breathing the air again now. How long before the particles build up again and I DO fall asleep?"

Big G looked grim as he set off down the corridor. "Don't know."

I followed him, dodging sleeping scientists. "How did you get so . . . well, *big*, just like that?"

"Just the way of things for my people. Little G was the child. Now Big G is the grown-up."

I scowled. "Because you ate my goldfish?"

"Did not EAT Herbert." Big G paused in the corridor, and I looked at him expectantly. "I LINKED to Herbert. He is alive and well, OK? Look, here on the TONGUE!"

Suddenly a long, rolled-up tongue unwound at speed from Big G's mouth, like a bright green party blower. But instead of a feather taped to the end, there was . . .

"Herbert?!" I cried.

"Greetings, Timothy," came a small, cheery voice, as the saliva around the goldfish bubbled. "This is all a bit of a surprise, isn't it?"

"Stop that!" I told Big G.

"Not me!" Big G insisted, speaking with his mouth open. "Your fish! He has learned to speak through Big G's tongue. OK? I knew tongue was ready for the linking because its smell had changed."

I had dissolved into a weirded-out bundle of disbelief. "*That's* why you kept saying 'I smell the tongue'?"

"Yes." Speaking with his tongue sticking out made Big G sound like a patient at the dentist's. "Tongue was ripe for the linking."

"It's wondrous!" I saw Herbert was actually attached to Big G's slobbery tongue. "This linking of our different forms is my *destiny*. Do you know what the G in Little G stood for, Timothy? GOLDFISH! Yes, this upstanding alien knew, deep down, that one day we would come together. He could sense certain future events – such as the hyper-beam sending *you* into space. That is why he always called you spaceboy. Now, you must hurry in your task – and I must go and meditate on my ever-growing intelligence. Cheerio!"

Big G's tongue rolled up like a roller blind, and he gulped my fish back down. Then he headed back off along the corridor.

"This is beyond freaky," I said bitterly, trailing after Big G. "How come the hyper-beam worked for me at all?"

"It is meant for children," Big G explained. "Hyper-beam adapted from Little G's personal travel-system. Big Suits thought Little G was dim, but Little G just a child! Not know so much. That's why it worked for you but not adults." He sighed, head drooping. "Tried to tell boss humans. Not OK. Did not know right words."

"Um . . . never mind." I gave him an awkward pat on the arm. "Can you *make* the beam work for adults, so we can wake up the Suits?"

"Already does!" Big G bobbed his head. "Now I'm smart, I fixed it easy – so grown-up G could come and get you! But we are not waking human adults. No way." He wrinkled his two noses like he'd smelled something bad. "They would not listen to Big G. They would mess things up worse."

"You mean things can *get* more messed up?"

Big G nodded gravely. "MUST wake Elodie, Ray and Kimmy. They built TAMASSISS suit. They must build it even better – and fast."

As we set off at a speedy walk/waddle, the thought struck me – like a hammer behind the ear – that right now, no one in the entire world was doing ANYTHING. Every person and animal on the planet would slowly starve in their sleep. How many homes and restaurants had burned down from cookers left on? What about all the drivers conking out at the wheel? What about the planes in the sky? How many billions of birds and flies had come down like a battering rain on the silent landscape?

And to think I'd thought that moving into the Rubbish House was the end of the world!

The Earth I knew now lay at perfect peace, waiting for its new owners to settle in. What fate awaited the creatures in the rivers and oceans? Would they be gulped down when the Ova-Many babies got thirsty? Or would Earth's waterways become vast alien bathrooms, filling steadily with indescribable wees and poos and sick-up?

As we reached the door to the Crèche, I looked at Big G and he seemed to know what I was thinking.

"Little hug now?" he murmured. "Hug, OK?"

It says something about my craving for comfort that I wrapped my arms around his alien neck and held on tight.

Then we went inside. Elodie, Kimmy and Ray were snoring softly, sprawled over their desks. I wondered numbly where Dad had fallen asleep – and my unexpected mum too. My instinct was to search them out – but what if they had blanked out on the toilet or something? Or naked in the shower? That would be seriously embarrassing.

In any case – all that would have to wait. Big G helped me drag Ray, Kimmy and Elodie to the hyper-beam room one by one. Then he set up a scanner so I could keep a filtered-eye on the alien spaceships hovering out past Mars. Were they tracking us down even now – the last two wakeful animals on the planet . . . ?

To keep my mind busy while we worked, Big G talked (with occasional contributions from Herbert) and I finally got my head round some stuff – which I present now in a stupendous comic strip format:

THE LIFE HISTORY OF LITTLE G

ON LITTLE G'S DISTANT WORLD, CHILDHOOD CAN LAST SEVERAL HUNDRED YEARS, AND CHILDREN CAN SOMETIMES SEE INTO THE FUTURE.

HELLO! HELLO, FUTURE! LITTLE G!

LITTLE G CAME FROM A FAMILY OF EXPLORERS WHOSE SPACESHIP DEVELOPED A FAULT IN OUR SOLAR SYSTEM.

UH-OH! A FAULT!

HUUGG! MMMM!

LITTLE G KNEW THAT EARTH BELONGED TO THE GETS AND WAS SURPRISED TO FIND HUMAN BEINGS IN CHARGE.

OH DEAR.

THE CHILDREN OF LITTLE G'S RACE GROW UP WHEN THEIR TONGUES TELL THEM THEY ARE READY TO 'BOND' WITH A SMARTER LIFE FORM.

MMMM, I SMELL THE TONGUE!

CAN YOU SMELL ME?

MINUTES AFTER BONDING, THE CHANGE BEGINS.

THIS IS FUN!

HELLO!

LITTLE G KNEW HUMANS WEREN'T CLEVER ENOUGH FOR HIM TO BOND WITH. BUT GOLDFISH . . . THEY WERE ANOTHER MATTER!

HELLO! COME TO PAPA!

"How come?" you might cry.

The answer was quite simple:

WHAT HAPPENED TO HERBERT?

SMELLS TRAVEL THROUGH WATER AS WELL AS AIR, AND THE **GETS'** PONGY MESSAGE ACCIDENTALLY MUTATED GOLDFISH BRAIN CELLS . . .

. . . CAUSING, OVER MANY MONTHS, UNUSUAL BEHAVIOUR AND VASTLY INCREASED INTELLIGENCE . . .

LOOK! I CAN DO TRICKS! WHEEEE!

RIGHT NOW, GOLDFISH ARE THE CLEVEREST CREATURES ON THE PLANET (CLOSELY FOLLOWED BY KOI CARP AND CERTAIN TYPES OF SQUID)

WHILE LINKED, BOTH LIFE FORMS SHARE EACH OTHER'S POWERS.

KA-ZAAAPP!

Elodie was the first to undergo Big G's brief tour of outer space. She came back, eyes wide and bulging, groaning and gasping for breath. Big G flopped down on the floor beside her in the TAMASSISS.

It was such a relief to see someone *not* sleeping. "Elodie, you're awake!"

"You could tell that just by looking, huh?" she said dryly. "Man, I had this awful, awful dream . . ."

"That every other person on Earth has been put to sleep by Giant Extra-Terrestrial stink machines? It's true!"

"No, that my estranged father didn't want to see me while my mother was all gooey over my dimwit brother," Elodie said meanly. "*That's* true too." She paused. "So. You OK, Tim? We thought you were dead for sure."

"It was a close one," I said, leaving the other stuff for now. "You don't know how close."

Kimmy was the next to be brought back to the land of the living. She came round with a high-pitched whine. "Ooooof." She clutched her ears. "Who turned my flippin' head inside out? Elodie? I don't care if we're friends, I'm still taking serious legal action against you."

"Welcome back, Kimmy," I said.

"Tim?" She sat up and grinned. "Hey! You're alive!"

"Thanks to your suit," I said truthfully.

"Who's inside it?" Her face darkened. "Who's wearing my flippin' suit? Ray, is that you?"

"No, it's taking Ray into outer space," I said, reassuringly.

Kimmy, for once, was lost for words. Unfortunately she soon found them again and went off on a foul-mouthed, panic-stricken, and legally questionable rant until Ray and her precious suit came back.

"Hey," said Ray weakly, pushing himself up on his elbows. "I think I'm OK. I *think*. Ow. It hurts to think – I think. OW!"

Elodie glared at me. "Explanations, Tim?"

"Hello." Big G took off the TAMASSISS helmet and Herbert burst out of his mouth like . . . like a slimy goldfish on the end of a long alien tongue.

"Greetings!" he squeaked.

"AAAAAUGHHH!" screamed Ray, Kimmy and Elodie, banging their heads as they jumped backwards and collided.

"OW!"

"OOF!"

"ARGH! I'M GONNA SUE YOU!"

"Four kids, an alien and a goldfish with a law suit," I muttered dismally over the ragbag racket. "All that's left to save a planet."

"Shhhh!" cried Herbert imperiously. Then I realised that a whispering, scratching sound had crept into the hyper-beam room. With a sick feeling I also realised that I had taken my eyes off the scanner showing the GET ship. It was pulsing now with strange light – as the GETs' monstrous, shadowy chittersnipes began to blur into existence all around us . . .

THIRTY -ONE

"Oh, man, no way!" cried Elodie, rubbing her head. "What the hell are those things?"

"Scary," I suggested, hauling Elodie quickly to her feet.

Ray boggled as the creatures grew darker, more solid. "Must be our imaginations . . ."

"Mass hallucination," Kimmy agreed.

"No. A mass of chittersnipes." I dragged them both into a standing position. "The GETs sent them. They chased me and Big G all over their spaceship."

Ray boggled some more. "They did *what*?"

"Big G?" Kimmy echoed. "Chittersnipes? Spaceships? How much did I miss?"

Big G had swallowed Herbert back down and was busy fiddling with some controls on the far wall. "The chittersnipes are GET slave animals, OK? Used by the GETs for pest control."

Ray nodded thoughtfully. "And we're the pests!"

"So, let's get out of here and shut the door on them," I said. "Like, now."

"Nearly done." Big G pulled wires from the wall, which spat sparks at his camouflage jacket. "OK! *Nearly* nearly done."

"Nearly done what?" I yelled, shoving Ray, Kimmy and Elodie towards the open doorway.

"Don't push me!" Elodie snapped.

"The chittersnipes were sent here by GET hyper-beam," Big G called over. "I am widening the range of *our* hyper-beam here so that as soon as they are solid, OK, I can project them back out into space."

Herbert burst out on his gloopy organic party blower. "That was my idea!"

"Ugh!" Kimmy complained. "You flippin' freak-fish!"

"Oi! That's my goldfish you're talking about," I told her, bundling her out of the door with Ray and Elodie. "Now, *shift*!"

"There!" Big G turned from his work, grabbed the TAMASSISS and bounded towards us, dragging it behind him. "Hyper-beam now on a ten-second timer. OK? Shoo!"

"Wait!" I gasped, even as the heavy door THUNKed shut behind him. "Sergeant Katzburger's still in there. Adults can't use the hyper-beam. She'll be killed!"

Elodie looked horrified. "We've got to get her out!"

SLAM! Something heavy and many-legged struck the door.

"Um, or not," said Kimmy quietly.

The chittersnipes had fully arrived on Earth. SLAM! SLAM!

"Those things are trying to bash their way out," said Ray. "We can't go back in there. We can't!"

The next moment it was irrelevant in any case. We heard the whooshing shoosh of the hyper-beam in operation . . . Bright red light flared under the door . . . The SLAM-SLAM-SLAMs grew fainter, then stopped – but the light glowed brighter still, until *then* . . .

BLAMMMM! That was the sound of something big and expensive blowing up.

"The hyper-beam must've blown a fuse," said Elodie, holding a hand to her chest.

Ray was gnawing his nails. "Were the chittersnipes sent back out into space?"

I hung my head. "What about Sergeant Katzburger?"

Big G boldly hit the keypad and the door clunked open. I peered tentatively inside.

The room was smoky, but empty. On the scanner, the GET ship had stopped pulsing.

"Power boost blew the contra-space funnel!" Big G groaned.

"We have spare parts in the Crèche!" Elodie was already racing away down the corridor. "We can track Katzburger down in space . . ."

We all chased after her. "Hurry!" puffed Big G, bundling the TAMASSISS above his head. "Hurry!"

"Hey!" Kimmy yelled. "You flippin' thief! Where you taking that?"

Big G shook his head. "You must fix the intangibility field in the suit so it's *stronger* – so it makes many transparent at once, not just someone right up close."

Kimmy gasped. "You want to mess with **PERFECTION?**"

"Come on," I told her, pulling her along.

By the time we'd caught up with Elodie and Ray, they were standing in front of the big screen, staring at empty space.

"Sergeant Katzburger was sent to this spot, just as we were," Elodie said slowly. "Even if we fixed the hyper-beam in time . . . there's no trace."

Ray took a deep, deep puff on his inhaler. "We've lost her."

It was an awful moment. I had a silent little cry for the miserable sergeant who'd had such bad luck with pets. Such bad luck full stop. Despite everything I wished Dad was there to hold on to. Instead he was asleep somewhere in the base, out of reach. Like my newfound mother . . .

And like every other person in the world.

Still, just then it was Katzburger filling my thoughts. The next chapter will be silent, as a mark of respect.

THIRTY -TWO

We all stared at the screen in silence.

Silently.

SILENCE! HAVE YOU NO FLIPPIN' RESPECT? HUH!

THIRTY -THREE

Once our minute's silence ended, we watched miserably as the alien ship shimmered and flickered even through the high-tech filter on the screen.

"This is all the fault of those GET things," said Elodie. "Just what ARE they?"

"They come from the Monnos galaxy, billions of light years away," Big G explained. "Such big beings need lots of space, like the Ova-Many – so they spread far and wide buying up property."

"Earth's their holiday home," I explained casually. "They said the last time they came here was about 350 million years ago."

"You've actually talked with those things . . ." Ray was looking at me with new respect. "What happened?"

"Work on suit!" Big G insisted. "Now you awake, you *must* boost the intangibility!"

So while Ray and Elodie helped Kimmy with Big G's improvements to the suit, I explained all that had happened in chapters twenty-seven to twenty-nine (without the pictures). I thought someone might comment on how brilliantly brave I'd been, surviving all that stuff without going totally mad. But the Crèche lot were maybe too busy working, and their curiosity was scientific as usual.

Elodie glanced up from the circuit she was building. "So it turns out that the GET ship is parked in front of another, way-larger ship – owned by the Ova-Many?"

"Yep," I said. "The big one's stuffed full of alien babies ready to move in."

"All those lights in the sky after the Big Miracle got rid of the pollution," Kimmy called, her legs sticking out through the neck of the TAMASSISS as she fiddled about inside. "They were prospective buyers, checking out the Earth!"

"But the GET sellers had a problem." Herbert burst out of Big G's mouth, surfing his tongue as it unfurled. "Under intergalactic law, the human race is a protected species – because you've lived on the planet for over two million years, you have squatter's rights."

"What's a squatter?" asked Kimmy.

"Someone who lives in someone else's property even though they don't own it," said Elodie, holding Ray's new improved fission chip up to the light for study. "Like, back in Ontario, if you stay in an unoccupied building for ten years, it's yours."

Ray put down a screwdriver. "So, even though the GETs see humans as nothing more than pests on their property, they can't just wipe us out. It's like if we get bats nesting in our roof, we can't just clear them out because they're protected by law. Like the natterjack toad and the great crested newt and the little whirlpool ram's-horn snail and—"

"And me!" cried Kimmy. "Protected by law! You'd better flippin' believe it!"

"Yes, OK, OK," said Big G. "Under galactic law, the GETs must get your agreement in writing for the sale to the Ova-Many to go ahead."

"But the human race would NEVER agree to that," Elodie pointed out.

"Of course not." Big G looked doleful. "But if the GETs can prove they've asked you, and that you have not bothered to reply within one Earth year, they can proceed with the sale without your consent."

"So, *that's* why the GET sellers filled the air with a tricksy coded message, even though they've learned perfect English," I realised. "They didn't *want* us to understand!"

"Indeed, Timothy!" Herbert popped out of Big G's mouth again like the cuckoo in a particularly fishy cuckoo clock. "The GETs scanned human technology levels and found the hyper-beam in operation. They knew full well that humans didn't really understand it – but it gave them the excuse to contact you in an advanced alien manner."

Kimmy peeped out from inside the suit to give Herbert a suspicious look. "How would you know, weirdo fish?"

"It was the GETs' amazing alien scents that transformed my meagre mind into a mighty organ," Herbert said grandly. "And since they communicate using smells in the air, I learned to do it too. That meant that when the GET building the stink machines was talking to his fellows back on the ship, I could pick up on some of their conversations – once the odours eventually reached my fish bowl."

I felt slightly hurt. "All that time I thought you were listening to me confiding all my troubles!"

"Er . . . well, yes, I was, Timothy." Herbert looked sheepish – if a fish *can* look sheepish. "And I was, er . . . most interested."

"I'll bet," said Elodie, yawning.

"Right." I looked at him doubtfully. "Well, anyway – in the end, we *did* translate the GETs' coded message, and made it to their ship. So by law, the GETs had to get human agreement to the sale."

"And obviously no president of a big power or whoever is just gonna agree to sign." Elodie slotted the finished fission chip into her circuit. "So the GETs prepared smelly illusions to trick him . . . to make him believe his biggest fears would come true if he didn't sign." She looked at Tim. "But instead of the president, they got you."

"Right." Kimmy took her friends' new, improved

lash-up and slotted it deep inside the workings of the suit. "Obviously, if they'd stinkified the *real* president, he would have seen stuff like nuclear wars, or the whole nation going up in smoke, or himself being sued. Serious grown-up stuff! Not rubbishy fears like the ones in Tim's head."

"Oi!" I protested – though I knew she was right.

"I guess it shows you're kind of scared of me, eh, bruv?" Elodie looked somewhat pleased. "I suppose you feel intimidated by my superior intelligence."

"Superior?" I scowled. "*Pooperior*, you mean!"

"Wow, I can see Dad must've loved living with someone so witty."

"I can see why Mum was so keen to meet someone normal like me instead of a stuck-up brain on legs like you!"

Herbert made another pop-out appearance on the super-tongue express. "Please! This is no time to argue."

"Don't fight, guys, please." Agitated, Ray took two puffs on his inhaler. "Elodie, Tim did really well. And Tim, Elodie's not just a brain on legs. She, er . . . has arms too."

Elodie rolled her eyes. "Thanks, Ray."

"The fact remains, Timothy," Herbert went on, "that you *did* sign a contract saying Earth was fair game for GET development."

"True," I cringed. "But . . . I'm not President, am I? It doesn't count."

"But the GETs don't know that!" Herbert shook his head on the gooey tongue. "That's why they sent chittersnipes here. They have to get hold of the signed contract."

I hid my face in my hands. "Their legal permission to end the human race . . ."

"Nice going, stupid," came Elodie's mutinous mutter.

"You'd have signed it too," I told her.

She shook her head. "I'd have used logic to resist their dumb illusions."

"Oh? Before or after you pooed your pants?"

"Pants," said a familiar voice from the Crèche doorway. "Yes, pants. I love pants. Let's talk about pants . . ."

Big G, Herbert, Ray, Kimmy, Elodie and I – we all

just stared.

There, swaying in the doorway – her hair spikier than ever and a weird, unnerving smile on her face – was Sergeant Katzburger.

"You won't believe what's happened to me," she murmured, walking slowly inside and shutting the door. "Please, now. Pants! Let me tell you all about it . . ."

THIRTY -FOUR

"Wow! Fantastic!" I started forward to hug Sergeant Katzburger, amazed she could possibly be alive. But she was smiling so hard her face looked ready to break. And I had never once seen her smile before.

Glancing around, I saw the others looked wary too.

"Sarge!" I said, suddenly awkward. "We, er, thought you were dead!"

"Dead? Me? Pants!" she cried, running a hand through her extra-spiky Mohawk, still smiling like a loon. "Of course I'm not dead. You guys are such pessimists!"

"*We're* pessimists?" murmured Ray, looking confused.

"How did you get back here?" asked Elodie.

"The GETs picked me up with the chittersnipes in space," said Katzburger. "I escaped using their hyper-beam when they weren't looking. Talk about getting away by the seat of my pants! Or, actually, just talk about pants."

"You've, um, had a bit of a shock," said Elodie. "Why don't you sit down?"

"She smells . . . different!" Herbert declared. "How did she survive the hyper-beam, hmm?"

"Oh, Little G, it was a piece of pants!" she said, ignoring Herbert's existence, totally unfazed. "Um, cake I mean. Piece of cake! Piece of pants cake!"

"*Little* G?" I echoed incredulously, some nasty suspicions forming. "Er, Sergeant, aren't you surprised to see him like this?" I gestured to Big G. "I mean, don't you see how he's changed . . . ?"

"Changed his pants?" Katzburger grinned again. "Well, I think I should check – don't you, everybody?"

Kimmy grimaced. "I think the hyper-beam has put you back together messed-up."

"Trash talk, missy! The GETs put me back together with their mega-alien technology, and they're too smart to mess up . . ." She trailed off. "Anyway, let's not talk about them. It's pants time! Someone's got something naughty in their pants, haven't they?"

"This," said Ray, anxiously, "is all kinds of wrong."

"She's American," Elodie reminded us. "Pants equals trousers."

"Pants!" Katzburger agreed.

Suddenly, it struck me – or rather, it crinkled damply against my butt-cheeks – that I had stuffed the GETs' sneaky agreement thing down the back of my trousers. Could Katzburger know that somehow? What if this wasn't the real Katzburger at all, but some kind of GET trick?

Playing a hunch, I grabbed some paper from the desk behind me and pretended to pull it from the back of my trousers.

"Hey, look what I found in my pants!" I cried.

"GIVE ME THAT," Katzburger screamed, lunging towards me and snatching the paper. "Ha! THERE! I have it, human-thing scum! I have the contract from your pants where we sensed it resided!" She laughed wildly. "Now, I shall be hyper-beamed back to the GET ship with it, and conversion of this world can proceed as planned."

She ran out of the room, leaving the rest of us in a stunned silence.

"Bad Katzbonker," Big G concluded.

"I told you she smelled funny!" Herbert squeaked. "The GETs must've rescued her scrambled body and put her back together to use against us!"

"Nice going, Tim." Elodie rounded on me. "You gave that bogus Katzburger the contract!"

"Actually, I didn't," I shot back. "I gave her an *equally* bogus blank bit of paper to expose her as a fake."

Kimmy considered. "Better than exposing our pants."

"That was quick thinking, Tim," said Ray kindly. "But how long before she realises she *hasn't* got the contract and—"

Suddenly the door burst open again. It was Katzburger – only this time she was holding a gun.

"OK, human-thing scumballs," she said brightly. "Hand over the REAL contract. Or I start shooting."

Elodie and I both spoke at the same time: "Do that, and you'll never find out where we hid it." We looked at each other in surprise, but this hardly seemed the right moment to link little fingers and say "Jinx".

"I know it's in this base somewhere," Katzburger warned us. "So tell me or, BOOM!" She pointed the pistol at Big G. "Gimme the contract. Now! Or ugly here gets it!"

Big G quickly opened his mouth and unrolled his tongue – practically pushing Herbert down the barrel of Katzburger's gun!

I gasped. "No!"

Herbert looked at Katzburger with the cutest, sweetest expression you could ever imagine.

"Please," he begged the burly soldier. "Can you really bring yourself to hurt an innocent pet like me?"

"Yes," said Katzburger.

"No!" wailed Herbert. "Remember how many lovely pets that you cared for died as the GETs flew overhead in search of subjects to study . . . Fate made you aware of their evil schemes . . . and now the GETs have abducted YOU . . . They are trying to make YOU kill a poor, helpless, teeny-weeny goldfish . . ."

Katzburger swallowed hard. She was sweating. "Con . . . tract . . . in pants . . ." she slurred. "They told . . . me in . . . my head . . ."

"Think of who you really are!" Herbert was staring into her eyes like a master goldfish hypnotist. "Sergeant Katzburger, who joined the army to *fight* nasty aliens . . . who pledged her life to defend Earth's pets. Every moment you delay us may lead to the death of a gorgeous fish, a lovely hamster, an innocent, fluffy little rabbit . . ." His voice became unexpectedly deep and spooky; Big G was talking in time with him. "Think of who you really are, Sergeant!

Fight the GETs' mental hold! **THINK! THIIIIIIIIIIIIIINK!**"

Katzburger groaned, dropped the gun, closed her eyes and collapsed with an almighty THUMP.

For a long moment, no one moved. Then we all released breaths we didn't know we were even holding.

"Is she dead?" I whispered.

Ray checked. "She's asleep," he said. "And . . . she's got a really miserable look on her face. That's got to be a good sign, right?"

"Wow," I said softly. "My goldfish **ROCKS!**"

"OK! OK!" Big G did a little wiggly dance, while Herbert did a weird attempt at a Mexican wave on his tongue.

"Uh-huh!" he squeaked. "I'm yo daddy!"

"Um, I hate to point out the obvious," said Elodie. "But if the Katzburger trick didn't work, the GETs are gonna try something else."

"What's next?" Ray muttered.

"I think I know," said Kimmy. "Almost certainly . . . legal action."

"Will you shut up about suing people all the time!"

I cried. "Never mind what the GETs are going to do. What are WE going to do about THEM? Somehow, we've got to find a way to scare them off. To show those aliens that this is our planet – and while we haven't exactly treated it nice, we're not gonna let them treat it worse."

"Nice speech," said Elodie. "But do you have even the foggiest idea of how we do that?"

"Er, yes!" I said defensively. "I . . . I'm going to ask Big G." I turned to him. "G, you can sense what might happen in the future, right? You told the guys to increase the intangibility field on the suit – what does that really mean?"

Ray took a portentous puff on his inhaler. "It's a matter of boosting the batteries so that not only is the suit and anything touching it intangible, but also part of the surrounding area."

I nodded, understanding. "So, Big G – why did you say to do that?"

The next moment, a horde of chittersnipes burst into the Crèche! Their eyes flashed, their teeth clacked together and their legs were a blur as they rushed towards us.

"OK!" Big G grabbed Ray and the unconscious Katzburger and hurled them towards the suit.

"Switch on, Kimmy!" Elodie shouted, and Kimmy swiftly stabbed a button inside the TAMASSISS . . .

I screamed as the chittersnipes pounced towards us – but my shriek died out into embarrassed coughing as the air turned speckled gold, and the hideous things passed through us as harmlessly as bullets through smoke.

"*That* is why I said to do that." Big G smiled and shrugged. "OK! I sensed this might happen. *That's* why!"

With the suit's powers boosted, we had ALL turned transparent. Even the furniture around us seemed no more solid than a hologram. Again and again, the chittersnipes tried to bite and swipe and snatch at us in the golden light. But there was nothing they could do.

"How long can we stay this way?" I asked.

"For about two hours," said Kimmy, "if the battery's fully charged."

I nodded hopefully. "And is it fully charged?"

"Nope. In fact, it's just about empty." Ray sighed. "I guess Big G's been using it quite a bit, and the intangibility engine eats up power, and—"

"Shhhh!" Elodie hissed, as the chittersnipes kept leaping and scuttling through and around us. "We don't know if those things can understand us!"

"What about Katzburger's gun?" said Kimmy. "When we turn solid again, we could shoot them!"

"There's too many of them," I said. "Anyway, what if they're bulletproof?"

"Perhaps we should run away?" Ray suggested.

"They'll just follow us," said Elodie and I together.

I turned to Big G hopefully. "Any more hints from peeking into the future?"

The alien shook his head and sighed. "I was child then, OK? Grown up now and can't see. Being grown up sucks! No fun."

"I heard that!" came an indistinct squeak from Herbert.

"Being a kid's not exactly a piece of cake right now, either," said Elodie. "Even super-smart kids like us."

"Wait! Wait a sec . . ." I frowned. "Gangsters!"

"Huh?" said Kimmy.

"Kimmy, you said you guys were like gangsters . . ." I cast my mind back. "Science was your gun, and intelligence was your other gun, right? You blackmailed the bosses here into letting you work, right? With antigravity pads and—"

"A bomb!" Ray punched the air. "That bomb I made, in case we had to blow up our work here to stop the military stealing it. It's in the cupboard under the sink!"

Elodie frowned. "Great! We can blow ourselves to bits. Cool!"

"Here it is!" Kimmy cried. We turned to find her pulling what looked like a random bundle of grey plasticine and wires from a cupboard. She gave her best nine-year-old snarl at the chittersnipes, who still bit and scratched the air around us. "You want a piece of this, huh? You want to taste Ray's bomb? Huh? HUH?"

"Watch out!" Elodie begged her. "It's caught up in our intangibility field. The blast won't touch them

– but it'll probably kill us!"

The golden light was starting to flicker.

"Oh, no. The battery's almost out." I closed my eyes. "In a few moments we'll be solid again with two messy choices – blow ourselves to bits, or let the chittersnipes tear us apart!"

THIRTY
-FIVE

Suddenly I felt a hand slip down the back of my trousers. *Whoa!* I thought, as the contract was whipped from out of my pants' waistband . . . By Sergeant Katzburger!

"I got it!" she yelled, running away, out of the intangibility field, through the door and into the corridor outside, away from sight. "I got it, I got it, come on!"

The chittersnipes started after her at once. Big G had been right – all they wanted was the contract.

"She got the bomb, too!" Kimmy gasped, staring at her empty hands. "She snatched it from me as she ran past! She got the flippin' bomb—!"

Ker-BLAMMM!

The whole place shook and evil black smoke billowed past the doorway.

"Hey, the bomb worked!" said Ray with some surprise.

"But . . . what did it do?" Elodie led the way over to the door. The smoke outside was clearing. Black chittersnipe gunge was scattered everywhere. Ray puffed on his inhaler, and kept the end in his mouth like it was a snorkel.

There was no sign of Katzburger . . . Until suddenly a panel in the ceiling fell to the ground, and a stocky figure dropped from the vent above.

"Katzbonker alive!" cried Big G.

"HA! FOOLED YOU!" Katzburger raged at the remains on the floor and walls. "The old 'throw-the-bomb-and-hide-in-a-vent-shaft' trick – ALIEN SCUM."

She glared at Big G. "Um, no offence, weirdo."

Big G nodded and smiled, then waddled off back into the Crèche.

I approached her warily. "Sergeant, are you back to normal?"

"Normal, kid? What's normal?" She shook her head bitterly. "Can any of us pretend we're normal, caught up in this crazy, senseless world of pain?"

"I think she's back to normal," Elodie confirmed.

I patted Katzburger's arm (I considered a hug, but she had bits of dead chittersnipe on her clothes and that put me off a bit). "Well, I guess we've started fighting back . . . But what can we do now?"

"This, for a start." Ray had ducked back inside the Crèche, and came out holding the sergeant's gun. "Here you go!"

"I feel better now we have our own one-woman army!" Kimmy held up a hand to Katzburger. "Respect, girlfriend!"

"Respect?" Katzburger curled her lip. "I don't want no respect. After what those GET things did to me, I want **REVENGE**."

"They rescued you from space and saved your life," Elodie pointed out. "Maybe they're not all bad. Maybe they really need the money they'll get for selling Earth – for an operation or something."

"Gee, you think we should maybe hold a collection for them?" Katzburger scowled. "I say we launch every nuke on Earth down their giant extraterrestrial throats!"

Elodie shook her head. "For all we know, the GETs eat nuclear missiles for breakfast. Besides, everyone else on Earth is asleep – including all the people in charge of nuclear weapons."

Katzburger was too busy frowning at Elodie to hear. "So what's YOUR plan, Miss Perfect Uptight-Buns?"

"Use our intelligence," said Elodie. "The GETs are our neighbours in space and crazily advanced. Words could be better than weapons! We need to convince them that we're more than just ants. That we matter! We need to make a noise about being human."

"Make a noise about being human," I repeated, a light bulb glimmering above my head. "That's it! Maybe words could BECOME weapons . . ."

My head was suddenly crowding with thoughts – the nasty neighbours who'd hated us and the Rubbish House, the complaints when I worked Dad's weirdo-scope in the garden all through the night . . .

Through the crowd of thoughts, a handsome, well-dressed idea was just beginning to stride with unexpectedly confident steps . . .

"Big G!" I ran back to the Crèche to find him standing quietly in the middle of the room. He looked a bit peaky, I thought, and his head was cocked to one side as if listening.

I burbled on regardless. "Remember when you saved me up on the GET ship? Remember how the GETs were hissing '*Silence them!*'—" I broke off. "How come you're so quiet now?"

"Vibrations," Big G said queasily. "Not OK! *NOT* OK."

Herbert sprang out on Big G's tongue like a fishy jack-in-the-box. "I can hear it coming – the GET that installed the stink machines, the one whose footprints you saw in the snow . . ."

I probably turned snowy white myself. "There's a *GET* coming **HERE? NOW?!**"

There are no words to summon the impossible, mind-maddening sound of rock and metal actually *tearing* as the GET began removing the roof of our underground secret base. I pictured how far Dad and I had descended into the frozen earth when we'd first arrived, hundreds of metres, surely . . .

And now suddenly those layers of ice, stone and steel were being peeled away as easily as a chimp could open a banana.

I heard Elodie's scream from the corridor outside. "Katzburger and the chittersnipes didn't work out . . . So now the GETs are gonna sort us out themselves!"

"Run for it!" Katzburger bellowed over the terrible, terrifying noise.

"This way!" Kimmy cried.

As for me, I barely had time to hide beneath a desk with Big G and Herbert as the ceiling above was snatched away and blinding, Arctic whiteness flooded in. Peering up I could see the ghostly, shimmering blur of the GET and what looked like a half a mountaintop being tossed into the distance.

"It's angry," Herbert squeaked. "Very, very angry!

And impatient! Very, *very* impatient!"

I thought of Dad, and Mum (MUM!), and then every person scattered around this base, asleep and now exposed to the twin dangers of extreme cold and extremely mad giant invisible alien invader.

And knew it was all my fault.

"Ooooh!" Herbert was looking up at me, alarm in his dark little eyes. "Look out, Timothy! It knows you're here!"

"Then . . ." I swallowed down the lump of raw fear in my throat, felt it scratch my insides all the way down, ". . . I guess . . . there's no point hiding." I scrambled out from beneath the desk and looked up.

"It's me you want!" I yelled. "I'm the President, remember! I'll sign anything you want, only . . ." I shivered violently. "Only put the roof back on, we're freezing!"

There was an awful, frigid silence broken only by the horrible, snow-choked howling of the wind. I caught a shimmer of light – the GET was up there somewhere.

"It can't hear you!" Herbert squeaked.

"But . . . it *must* be able to hear me!" I yelled. "Its mates were telling me to shush at the tiniest thing before."

"It's saying . . . it can't hear you over the others," Herbert went on. "It's grumbling about the awful noise human things make."

"What?" I didn't understand what the GET was on about – I couldn't hear the others at all. Had it gone after them instead of me? A firework of fear exploded in my stomach.

"Whoa!" Herbert gasped. "Ooh, NOW the GET knows where you are . . . !"

A deep, sinister whisper hurt my ears. "It is time this foolery was ended."

I sensed rather than saw the impossible, giant hand sweeping down through the white sky towards me.

THIRTY -SIX

I stared up, too dazed and horrified even to comprehend how close to death I must be . . .

Suddenly an enormous jet aircraft rose swiftly and silently from the exposed base and slammed into the blur of air above me! It was quickly followed by dozens of spiky satellites, then a couple of Chinook helicopters, and finally a humungous Stratolaunch carrier that came whooshing up from the base and smashed against the GET's body. I caught only the scariest glimpse of his sprawling, many-limbed form, wearing the high-tech hardware like so many badges.

Then their rise into the air continued, lifting the GET as they went.

"Oho!" squeaked Herbert. "Ooh, it's mad now! But it can't stop itself rising up into the air! Ooooh, it'll go up, up, up and into space!"

"But how . . . ?" I broke off and answered my own question. "Kimmy's antigravity discs! YES! She said they'd wired them underneath the planes and stuff to—"

"—blackmail the Big Suits into giving us proper resources," said Elodie, running up behind me. "And aren't you glad they couldn't take them off again, eh?"

"You're OK!" I grabbed her by the elbows as the wind chilled through me – then let go, self-consciously. "Um, is *everyone* OK? Apart from freezing to death, that is."

"No one's allowed the luxury of death until we beat those alien slimeballs," growled Sergeant Katzburger, striding into the room with a big pile of spacesuits. "C'mon kids. Get these on."

"The latest super-thermal design!" said Ray breathlessly behind her, his movements jerky with nervous excitement.

"But we can't put them on *everybody* in the base," said Kimmy, following on and already wearing her own oversized spacesuit minus the helmet. "The roof came off cleanly but now there will be casualties from the cold."

"Big Blanket . . ." said Big G from beneath the table. He looked poorlier now.

"You OK?" I asked him. "Did the GETs do something to you?"

"OK," Big G insisted.

"It's probably just the cold, eh?" said Elodie.

Big G smiled bravely. "Use antigravs . . . Lift it over base . . ."

"An artificial roof!" Ray nodded as he climbed into a spacesuit. "Sergeant Katzburger, can you let us into the Experimental Wing? The Big Blanket's been cut into smaller sections for study there – we can set more antigravity discs to support them at low level . . . Shouldn't take long."

"It'll keep the warmth in and it's pretty well impregnable!" Elodie grinned. "Best of all, it's using the aliens' own technology against them. I love it."

"And MY technology," Kimmy reminded her, waving an antigrav disc. "Don't forget whose flippin' technology it is!"

"Yeah, well, don't get too excited about it," said Katzburger, brushing snow from her uniform. "Something will probably go wrong in any case . . ."

She led Kimmy and Ray out of the Crèche, ready to raise the roof. Could they really put the lid back on this place and save us all? It was a question I kept to myself. Elodie would no doubt snipe at me, and Big G was in no state to speculate in any case. He was looking greener than ever, his eyes half closed, and he smelled like a leak in a fart factory.

"What is it, G?" I said, struggling to get into my own spacesuit. "*Is* it the cold . . . or are you sick?"

"Hello," said Big G, shivering. "Not right. Tongue not right. Hello." He shook his head. "Not right . . ."

"Oh, dear." Herbert sighed. "I fear this is my fault. Big G linked with me because goldfish are so smart now – but that's only because we absorbed the GETs' particles so quickly. I suspect my biology has begun to disagree with *his* biology."

I struggled to get my head round it. "You mean you've kind of given his body all-over indigestion?"

"A rather simplistic summary," said Herbert primly. "But close enough. It has, shall we say, badly upset his metabolism – and made his leap into adulthood unstable."

"Huuugggg," said Big G, pathetically, as I leaned in for a gentle, slightly whiffy embrace. "Mmmmm. Huuugggg."

"So will you have to leave him, Herbert?" asked Elodie. "Go back to your bowl?"

"I . . . I don't know." Herbert looked troubled. "I've been learning so much from Big G. My powers have increased enormously! But perhaps you're right. Perhaps I have grown big and wise enough to move on alone."

"Who said growing up was easy, eh?" said Elodie dryly.

"Dad's told me a hundred times that saving the world was the duty of the young." I shook my head. "I'm not sure he meant it quite like this." I took hold of Big G's hand. "Come on, fella. We need everyone in the zone if we're going to stand even the tiniest chance of doing this."

"We need help," Elodie agreed. "Resources. We have to find an antidote to this lullaby stink and wake up the world, quick!"

"Your plan, spaceboy . . ." Big G said quietly. "You were telling your plan . . ."

"That?" I shrugged self-consciously. "Oh . . . it's probably stupid. I just thought that instead of trying to stop the GETs selling the Earth, what if we could put off the Ova-Many from *buying* it?"

Elodie stared at me, and I could almost hear the data servers in her head humming as she considered the proposal. "Turn words into weapons, you said before . . ."

"Right." I looked straight at her. "House sales fall through all the time, don't they? Buyers get put off by stuff. I mean — what if you found out the place you wanted to buy had really annoying—"

"Noisy neighbours!" she joined in to finish my thought. "Of course!"

"Herbert's heard the GETs moaning about the noise we make," I said. "And the Ova-Many babies must be *really* sensitive to sounds, or they wouldn't need the lullaby stink in the air to soothe them."

"But how can we make *enough* noise?" asked Elodie. "To be a noisy neighbour to Earth, we'd have to be somewhere close by in space. We'd have to be on . . ."

"THE MOON!" we said together.

I looked at her. "We could, couldn't we? We could hyper-beam to the Moon . . . !"

Elodie shook her head. "Sound can't travel in a vacuum – the vibrations need air to carry them. And as you might just remember, there's no air in space." She shivered as another freezing gust blew biting snow all about us. "Whatever noise we made on the Moon, the GETs would never hear it."

"Ah, but the GETs do not hear things as we do!" Herbert piped up. "They translate and smell the *feelings* behind the words rather than the words themselves."

"Of course!" I breathed. "That explains why the GETs were saying to me, 'Silence!' when I wasn't even saying anything. And why they put up an 'emo-shield' thing when I was thinking how scared I was."

"Emo?" Elodie smiled triumphantly. "That'll be 'emo' as in 'emotion', then!"

"Yes!" I clicked my fingers – or tried to, in my thermal gloves. "Yeah, I bet that's it! Emotions!"

"Well," she said, "if you were anything like as scared as I was when the roof came off, we must've deafened that particular GET."

"We did! Herbert said we did!" But my sudden excitement was short-lived. "Er, hang on, though . . . How far away is the Moon?"

Elodie didn't hesitate: "About 384,400 kilometres from Earth, and over 80 million kilometres from Mars."

I groaned. "But the GETs are orbiting out past there. They'll never hear us, or smell us, or sense us, whatever we do."

"Not unless we make the words *louder*," said Herbert. "Amplify them in some way . . ."

"Hurry," said Big G faintly. "Must hurry."

"Yes, it will take time to prepare the right equipment." Herbert cleared his fishy throat. "I believe that right now, the GET sellers are having an urgent meeting with their Ova-Many buyers. Yes . . ." He narrowed his eyes and strained – he was either trying to listen in to the alien convo, or doing a poo (I hoped it was the former as Big G was looking pretty rough already). "The Ova-Many are concerned that a human thing and an unidentified life form broke into their ship and disturbed their babies . . ."

"That's you and me, Big G!" I spoke encouragingly, but his eyes were closed.

And suddenly, so was the roof. The wind had died and the epic wilderness vanished. A blurry sheet of nothingness hovered overhead.

"I guess Ray, Kimmy and the Sarge must've done it, eh?" said Elodie. "Big Blanket in position."

"Yes, but now our contact with the GETs has been lost." Herbert's eyes reopened. "The Big Blanket turns energy back on itself – my probing thoughts cannot penetrate their sensory network."

"Well, let's hope it's different on the Moon," I said, placing a gloved hand on Big G's forehead. "We've got to disturb those GETs again."

Herbert nodded. "I shall tell you how we can bring this about."

"We're all ears," I assured him. "I only wish the GETs were too – it would make things a lot easier."

Elodie gritted her teeth. "I have a feeling that easy is the *last* thing this is going to be."

And as Herbert explained what had to be done, I realised Elodie had just made the understatement of the century . . .

PART THREE

THE MOON

(Because I did say I really wanted there to be a **PART THREE**, and frankly, if we delay any longer it's not going to happen.)

THIRTY -SEVEN

Just six short, nerve-wracking hours later, I was standing on the Moon.

About here.

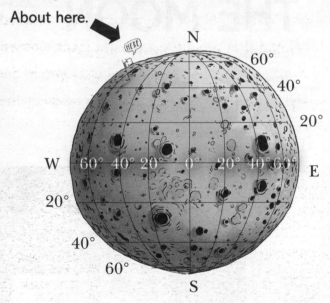

The hyper-beam had taken me from one north pole to another.

After my scary moments in space, I thought I'd probably cope OK on the Moon. But to stand on that shining grey dust, with nothing but barren wasteland and darkness all about, made me feel tiny and lost and lonely.

But, no. I couldn't let myself think that way. Our Mission had got to work.

I fought to keep my breath steady, a regular "shush" in my ears. The helmet got fogged up if you breathed too hard, and that was no good. And I was worried that if I got any sudden shocks, I would jump in the air – which, on the Moon, with only one-sixth the gravity of Earth, could be a big mistake.

Staring out at the dark magnificence of space, I saw Earth. I know proper astronauts in decades past called it the blue marble, and that's just what it looked like. White streaks of cloud trailed its surface, allowing only glimpses of land beneath, and a bandana of shadow hid its lower reaches from sight.

It looked fragile and solitary in the darkness.

"Know how you feel," I muttered.

"Huh?" Elodie's voice crackled into my helmet. She was crouched just behind me, carefully fiddling with a mess of wires, solar panels and scientific debris. "What did you say?"

"Nothing," I said.

Back on Earth, while Sergeant Katzburger was playing army medic, checking the base for anyone injured in their sleep, Ray and Kimmy were working on a way to reverse the GETs' stinky work by creating "wake-up" particles.

And most heroically of all, Big G was refusing to take his illness lying down. He was taking it on a stepladder, forcing himself to fix the blown fuse on the hyper-beam — a vital escape route if the GETs returned to the base to get our little gang.

I wished I could help him. But I couldn't really help anyone. I was only here to get myself used to being on the Moon.

"Your time to shine will come, Timothy," said Herbert, as if reading my mind.

There he was, my goldfish – the first fish on the Moon. Reluctantly, Herbert had agreed to leave Big G's tongue and go back to his bowl. Under his direction, Elodie, Ray and Kimmy had souped it up for space travel. They'd made it airtight, and fitted it with a heater, a water-recycling unit, a built-in radio microphone, even a glowing-effect artificial jellyfish for illumination.

And now, from this superbowl, he was bossing Elodie about in her titanically technical tasks.

We had come to this precise location – half way up a nameless mountain – because it was the crash site for two near-identical spacecraft, Ebb and Flow. These clever machines, each about the size of a washing machine, had been sent up by NASA in 2011 to map the gravitational field of the Moon. At the end of their successful mission – **SPLATT!** – the craft had been programmed to smack down into the lunar surface.

Big G had been around for the launch and knew what equipment the craft had been carrying. And though he might have been delirious, he reckoned we could combine their remains into a kind of celestial solar-powered sound system, specially designed to aggravate the GETs. Of course, we couldn't play music like this was a real party – phat beats and pounding basslines would mean little to GET ears, so we just had to think about our precarious position and turn our terror into something we could *use*.

I have to say, standing here, so vulnerable in this vast, eerie moonscape, was giving me plenty of potential.

"Right," said Elodie, screwing a thick red wire into a terminal on a cracked solar panel. "I've linked the S-band transponder antennas to the X-band beacon antennas. The emo-converters should now concentrate our thoughts and feelings, and the power boosters will fire the output straight at the

Ova-Many ship." She put down her tools. "Guys, we have ourselves a handmade emoto-audio wave-blaster."

I gave her a short round of applause which came out pretty rubbish in thermal gauntlets.

"Have the sellers and the buyers finished their meeting?" I wondered.

Herbert spun about in his bowl. "I am not sure. Stuck in this bowl I feel rather clumsy, my powers somewhat curtailed . . ." He sighed. "As a fish in water, I feel like a fish out of water. O! What bitter irony!"

"Hold those bad thoughts," I told him. "You can add your voice to ours."

"Shall we get started?" Elodie asked.

"We'd better," said Herbert.

"Right, then." I cleared my throat. My voice sounded weird and hollow, coming back at me inside the helmet. "Testing. Testing." My mouth was dry – I was feeling the pressure. Was I going to mess everything up?

That was as good a place to start as any. "I'm,

er . . ." I swallowed. "I'm kind of scared I'm going to be rubbish."

Herbert was studying his lunar lash-up. "Splendid. The wave-blaster picked that up. Go on."

"Um . . . I'm scared too, actually," said Elodie, loud and clear in my helmet receiver. "This whole situation is, like, *totally* scary."

None of us spoke for a few seconds.

"Keep it going, then!" Herbert coached us. "Explore your feelings."

"Er . . ." I sighed. "I don't have a lot of experience of that. Dad's never had a whole lot of time for feelings."

"Mum neither," said Elodie. "She's kind of trained me never to show any. Convinced me it's best not to get involved with anyone."

"Dad tried to do the same with me." I shook my head crossly. "What are our parents like? What happened to make them that way? What happened to make them want to make *us* this way?"

"Mum never really talked about it." Elodie puffed out a breath. "Look, we may not get a chance to talk about this later, and at least through this visor you can't see me blushing, so . . . Tim? I just wanted to say . . . Well, I'm sorry I was mean to you before. When you and your dad showed, when I realised who you were . . . I guess I freaked. I'm used to science and math and equations – you know, everything's got an answer, everything's exact. But dealing with stuff where the answer is just **'AUUUGHHHH!'** . . ."

I nodded. I had to nod my whole body like a Teletubby so she'd know. "Well, most of my life has been kind of **'AUUUGHHHH!'**, and I didn't handle things any better."

"I always knew I had a brother somewhere, like I knew I had a dad. But the thought of actually meeting you both after so many years – it was too much."

"Keep going!" Herbert urged her. "The machine is working, it's picking up your signals and transmitting them!"

"Noisy neighbours are go," I cried.

"More like soppy neighbours." Elodie stuck out her tongue. "Enough of that. We need to make some real noise here, eh? Get angry."

"OK," I said, reaching inside myself to see what I could take. "You know what makes me angry? My whole life! Whenever I'm hungry, Dad tries to give me home-grown organic cucumber. Any time of day. Sometimes he even tries to give me cucumber for pudding. Only, get this – he calls it 'cumber of cu'."

"Cumber of cu?" Elodie repeated, incredulous. "Truly?"

"He even writes poems about them. 'My love is ever true / for my sweet Cumber of Cu . . .'"

"Mum's obsession is tomatoes. I say, 'Mum, I want chocolate!' 'Have a tomato,' she says. And I'm like, 'Mum, I don't want a tomato, I'm totally sick of tomatoes.' And she's like, 'OK, dear, better have *three* tomatoes so your body learns to love them.'" Suddenly Elodie yelled at the top of her lungs, "Mum, **SHUT UP GOING ON ABOUT TOMATOES THE WHOLE TIME! I HATE YOUR DUMB TOMATOES!**"

I laughed. "Yeah, well, get this! Dad refused to even admit I had a mother, let alone a sister. He said I'd been brought into the world by aliens."

"No way!" Elodie sounded genuinely shaken. "He never told you a thing about us? That is so lame!"

"Totally lame, I know. Deep down, I've always half believed I belonged on another world." I stared around me at the harsh, alien landscape, its blanks and blacknesses. "At least now I know *that's* total rubbish." I gazed back towards Earth. "That's where I belong. I only hope we can actually pull this off."

But then a squawk of static broke inside my helmet. "Moon guys, this is Earth Base," Kimmy's voice crackled. "Those alien ships are on the move. Both of them."

"Flying off?" said Elodie hopefully. "We're driving them away?" There was a tense couple of seconds' pause.

"No," said Kimmy. "They're flying straight for you."

THIRTY -EIGHT

"I was afraid of this," Herbert cried.

"Not as afraid as me," I assured him. "You know that saying, 'about as popular as a fart in a spacesuit'? I'm putting it to the test. Does the emoto-audio wave-blaster pick up farts too?"

"I'm putting so much fear into it," said Elodie, "I can't believe it hasn't blown a fuse."

"Far from it," said Herbert. "It's not enough. Not enough!"

Flustered, I turned to Elodie. "How long do we have before the GETs and the Ova-Many get here?"

"Can't be long." She sounded close to tears. "Oh, Tim. I really thought this might work, but it hasn't, has it?"

"It was my stupid plan," I said.

"We're not beaten yet." Then Herbert pressed a

button in his supertank. "Goldfish to Katzburger! Has Big G fixed the hyper-beam?"

"Not finished testing yet," came her gruff crackle. "He's probably messed it up."

"You must use it now," Herbert commanded. "Quickly, Sergeant – bring on the big guns!"

"What big guns?" I stared at him. "Herbert, shouldn't we hyper-beam back to Earth?"

But the red glow stealing into the lunar landscape told me the hyper-beam was in use. Moments later, the bulky form of Sergeant Katzburger appeared, with a man and a woman – all three wearing spacesuits. But the man and the woman were too big to be Ray and Kimmy, so . . . ?

Katzburger grunted. "Here you go."

The man was swaying about, like he might collapse at any moment. "I was so tired . . . in the sick bay, then space . . . and suddenly I'm on the *Moon*?"

"Dad!" I squeaked in surprise. "You're awake! You're OK!"

"Better than OK – I've travelled to the Moon in no time at all and it didn't hurt the environment one little bit!" He tried to do a dance, but it was total rubbish and he stopped almost immediately.

"Elodie! Tim!" came a female voice.

"Mum!" shouted Elodie. "It's you!"

"Mum." The word sounded so strange in my dry throat, no matter how many times I said it. "Mum-mum-mum-mum. Mu*mmmm*. MUMM—"

"Yeah, well, I gotta go now," said Katzburger grimly. "Things to do. Crazy things that almost certainly won't work out. But at least it keeps us busy while we wait for our doom, right?"

I barely noticed the red flare of the sergeant leaving. My eyes were now firmly fixed on Dad, Hannah-Anna Hongananner and Elodie.

"Eric," said my MUM, "I don't want to bring you down, but this Moon business has got to be a hallucination, hasn't it?"

"I hope you're a hallucination too," said Dad.

Elodie looked down at Herbert. "Why did you bring them here?"

"It takes more than two people to get a party pumping!" Herbert was zipping first one way, then another. "You must go for it, together! Party hearty!"

"This is just crazy." Elodie was looking at Dad – *her* dad as well as mine – and shaking her head in wonder. "I mean, perfect time and place for a reunion, eh? NOT."

"Precisely!" Herbert cried. "Come along now, quickly! Share your pain! Confess your weaknesses! Tell your tales! Distribute the complexity of your emotions amongst the group, at once. DO IT! You may never get another chance!"

Luckily, neither Dad nor Hannah-Anna – I mean, MUM – paid the talking goldfish much attention at that point. Maybe his amazing alien fish-powers meant he could choose who heard him.

Or maybe, just maybe, Mum and Dad were finally thinking more about their children right now.

"Come here, Tim," said my mum. "I don't care if this *is* a dream. Oh my darling, let me look at you . . ."

I'm in a spacesuit, I thought dully. *You can't see a lot.* But nevertheless, she was pulling me in for a hug. I didn't hug her back. I froze. Then—

"No!" Dad pulled me the other way, so hard that I

almost fell over. "I'm not having you hug MY son, not even in a hallucination."

"He's my son too," said Mum.

"Dad!" Elodie sounded close to tears. "Don't you want to hug *me*?"

"I'm afraid I don't do hugs," said Dad gruffly.

There were half-developed hugs happening all over the Moon. What kind of rubbish, soppy astronauts were we?

But Herbert seemed pleased, shouting out like a director calling the shots. "Yes! More emotion! More drama! Yes, I say!"

"OK. I guess we really do need to talk – for Earth *and* for ourselves." I crossed carefully to stand beside Elodie and looked at Mum. "All right. How come I never got to know you?"

Elodie nodded and turned to Dad. "And why did I never get to know *you*?"

There was a tense pause. How close would the GET ship be by now?

Mum turned to Dad. "You know, this whole bare, hostile Moonscape is most likely a role-play scenario invented by either your subconscious or mine."

"Where the perceived threat of imminent catastrophe forces us to come to terms with unresolved personal traumas?" Dad suggested. "Interesting . . ."

Elodie leaned into me. "I can't think what first attracted them to each other."

"Very well." Dad took a deep breath and turned to Elodie. "Your mother and I both cared deeply about our work—"

"You cared more deeply about work than you did for me," Mum suggested.

"That's the test-tube-over-a-bunsen-flame calling the distillation vessel heated!" Dad retorted.

"If you mean, 'that's the pot calling the kettle black', say so," I begged. "Just so I can follow."

"We hoped having children would bring us together," Dad went on. "But no. We had fallen out of love—"

"You decided that very quickly," said Mum.

"—and it became obvious we would have to split up."

I looked at Elodie; I couldn't see her face through the helmet but I guessed she was wearing a look that said, *"So, it's our fault!"* I knew I was.

Mum sighed. "We wrangled over custody for weeks. In the end, to take one child each seemed fairest. To leave and sever all connection."

"Very mathematical," I muttered. "But, Dad, why did you never ever mention Mum and Elodie? Why pretend they didn't exist?"

Dad didn't speak for a few moments. His fists were clenched. He was starting to shake. Finally, like a skinny, middle-aged volcano in a spacesuit, Dad erupted at last. "Because Dr Hongananner left when you and Elodie were only six months old and it almost **KILLED** me!" he roared. "She broke my heart into a thousand tiny pieces! Then she got a hammer and **SMASHED** each one of those thousand tiny pieces of my heart into *ten* thousand even tinier pieces! Then she meticulously collected each of those ten thousand even tinier pieces, got a **SUBATOMIC LASER** and **BLASTED** each one of *them* into **TEN THOUSAND MILLION** pieces, some of which she **DISSOLVED** with **ACID**, some of which she **INCINERATED WITH A FLAMETHROWER** and several more of which she **FLUSHED** down a **DIRTY TOILET** that she then **BLEW UP WITH HER OWN BARE HANDS** and **DANCED** up and down on the last **CHARRED TRACES** before moving away to **CANADA!!!**"

I'd never seen him like that before. And I was so shocked by the outburst, by Dad acting like a human being (a kind-of-scary one, but even so), that I forgot where we were and what we were meant to be doing and how little time we maybe had in which to do it. Talking now, and talking properly, was suddenly all that mattered.

I squared up to Dad in the low gravity. "So you just forgot them? Wiped the muck from your shoes and kept on walking?"

"We agreed, no contact," said Dad. "It would have been too painful."

"He was always better at walking than talking," said Mum wistfully.

"I felt like a cracked bottle that's been chucked in the trash instead of recycled." Suddenly the old Dad was back, calm and considered. "So I took myself out of the Dustbin of Heartbreak and rolled along to the Recycling Plant of Second Chances. My broken shell was melted down and reformed in the white heat of a new and challenging job at the Space Centre, and my quest for a non-polluting form of space travel filled me with the Invigorating Liquid of Fresh Purpose . . ."

"You're not a recycled bottle, Dad," Elodie said hotly. "You're a person!"

"And you never could see, my poor dear . . ." Mum walked over to him. "Things that break don't always have to be recycled. Sometimes you can try to put them back together."

"Sometimes," said Elodie, regret thick in her voice. "But not right now."

I followed her line of sight, into a colossal blurring of the stars and the blackness. And felt a familiar sick feeling gnaw deep into my guts.

"The aliens," I murmured. "They're here."

Dad touched Mum's hand. "I must congratulate one of us on the realism of this imaginary situation," he said. "It's as if we really were about to face death at the hands of Giant Extra-Terrestrials . . ."

"Yup," said Elodie. "That's because we really are, Dad."

"That consequence-free environment you mentioned?" I said huskily. "I'm afraid it really does have consequences."

"AAUUGHHHHHH!" Dad yelled.

"Thank you, Professor Gooseheart, for that last cry of despair," Herbert piped up, keenly watching the shimmering blur overhead. "Well done, everybody. This is the Ova-Many's ship, with the alien nursery on board. I do believe we've got their attention."

"Enough!" came a voice up close in my head – in all our heads, I'd later learn. It was a whisper like before, but it sounded more exasperated than sinister. "For creatures small as dust you are so ridiculously noisy! Illogical and shouty. Annoying and caring and extraordinary. Clinging together even as you pull apart. Worried and loud and hopeful and rebellious and forgiving and . . . strong."

I licked my dry lips, looking up at the shimmering vessel. "That's . . . That's just how we are."

"Human things, you mean?"

"No." There was the tiniest tremble in Elodie's voice as she glanced at me, then back up at the stars. "Family."

"You understand family, don't you!" called Herbert imperiously, swishing his tail towards the blue marble in the sky. "And you must understand, that world you wish to purchase is *teeming* with families like this one. Millions and millions, swarming like dust motes in their little patch of sunlight. Would you allow your little ones to prosper by silencing so many others forever, hmm? Or would you travel elsewhere, to a naturally silent world that is owned and watched over responsibly – HMMM?"

It seemed as though that silence had already fallen. The vast, blurring reach of the Ova-Many craft still hung in front of us, striking upward as far as my eyes could see.

And then, swift as a sigh, it was gone.

The shushing of breath in our helmets was the only sound for quite some time, as Elodie and I waited for our wary minds to accept as fact what we dared to hope in our hearts.

"We did it," I whispered.

"We did it," Elodie whispered back.

Herbert swished around, looking pleased with himself. "I was rather good, wasn't I?"

Then Dad pointed at the bowl. "Ohhhh!" he said, as if some great realisation had just sunk in. "It was the *goldfish* talking." He laughed. "What a ridiculous hallucination this is!"

"I'm almost starting to enjoy it," Mum agreed.

Elodie laughed out loud, and I found myself wanting to join in.

I wish that I could just end things at this point. It would be neat, wouldn't it?

Thing was, there was still the GET ship out there. The ship full of very angry GETs who'd gone to so much trouble to sell the Earth . . . and whose would-be buyers were now thoroughly put off and heading for the other side of the galaxy.

In a heartbeat, there it was – the GET's spaceship, a shifting mass of bleary detail before us. Slowly it hardened to a solid, sinister cluster of creepy alien shapes . . .

"OK, it is deffo time to get out of here!" I shouted. "Back to Earth, Herbert! Come on!"

"Please!" cried Elodie.

But Herbert only stared, wide-eyed, at the terrifying sight becoming clear before us.

A colossal gun – it *had* to be a gun – was protruding from the middle of the spaceship. And the tip of the gun glowed with a terrible light – a light that grew bigger and fiercer – and then streaked towards us.

A death ray. Had to be.

I watched the end coming. We'd come so far in so many ways. But now it was all over.

Now, we were **DOOMED**.

THIRTY -NINE

At least, we *would* have been doomed . . .

Except, just then, in a blur of red light, four more suited figures appeared, floating in space above the lunar horizon, each a long, long way apart. If you could draw lines through space to join the little figures you would connect the corners of a massive rectangle.

I recognised Big G in the yellow TAMASSIS first, top left. Katzburger was top right, Kimmy far beneath her, and Ray wobbling about bottom left.

What was this, some kind of last salute?

Each was standing on an antigravity disc. Each was holding on to something blurry and dark.

My eyes made sense of it all at last: together they were holding up the *Big Blanket*! So big that it blotted out the gun and the fearsome fireball scorching through space towards us.

"**GENIUS!**" Elodie yelled. "The Blanket reflects energy, remember, like Herbert said! And that death-ray the GETs fired at us is energy too. So if the Blanket is only strong enough, then—"

My heart leapt. "It'll reflect the power back at them?"

"Zap!" Elodie agreed.

Then words died away as an enormous, soundless explosion engulfed the heavens around us. A storm of colours and shades burst from the great bulk of the GET ship, and whispers rushed past our ears like an impossible gale.

Then sound and colour were gone. As our friends released what was left of the Big Blanket and used their antigravs to drift down towards us on the lunar highlands, there was only endless space and stars above us.

Mum and Dad fell into each other's arms. Then they slumped to the dusty lunar surface, apparently in a dead faint. I watched them with a pang of jealousy. Oh, to just drop out of the whole situation and let someone else take care of it all!

"The GETs," I breathed. "Have they flown away or—"

"Their ship has been destroyed," said Herbert, and he sounded almost sad. "The destructive powers they unleashed upon us were turned back against themselves."

"Thanks to our friends," said Elodie, "coming to the rescue at the last possible second."

"Quit your lip, Uptight-Buns!" Katzburger growled as she landed. "We actually showed up at the *second-to*-last possible second." Suddenly, she grinned. "Timing is everything, right?"

"But how did you know when to arrive or what to do?" I asked, as the TAMASSISS landed beside me. "Big G can't see into the future now that he's grown up, can he—?"

"HELLO! Hello! Little G." The yellow-suited figure grabbed me in a clumsy embrace. "Mmmm! Hug! Hello!"

"*Little* G?" I exclaimed, trying to wriggle free.

"Hello!" He bounced into the air with me, a huge, exuberant leap. "Little G in little *G-force*! HELLO!"

"But how?" As I yelled down to the others, I found I was grinning my face off. "How come he's changed again?"

"Isn't that obvious?" fussed Herbert. "His body rejected the link with me, thanks to the conflicting alien cells in my system. So now he's returned to his childhood state."

"Huuugggg!" Little G was still trying to grab me in mid air like an over-playful puppy. "Hello!"

"Careful!" I yelled. "You'll put a hole in my spacesuit!"

"You can always sue him!" Kimmy called up to us. "Once the rest of the world has woken up, that is."

"Which they *will*," said Ray proudly. "Kimmy and I mixed up a handy-dandy chemical cure using 101 medicines and the Yellow Downpour as a base – highly diluted of course."

"That's what we used to wake your mum and dad!" Kimmy added.

I came down to Moon with a scuffling crunch, clinging on to Little G to stop me falling. "You mean, you broke the lullaby effect by feeding them a cocktail of drugs and alien baby sick?"

Elodie looked at our parents' sprawled figures and laughed out loud. "Good job, guys!"

"You bet your sweet legal fees it was," said Kimmy. "Now all we need do is prepare a powdered cure, synthesise the antidote for mass production, and load it into the GETs' stink machines. Instead of the lullaby, they will spit out a wake-up call!"

Ray nodded. "The human race should start stirring pretty much straight away."

"In time to feed their fish and small furry friends," said Katzburger, "and walk their dogs. And change their kitties' kitty litter. And put nuts in their bird feeders. And place lettuce leaves in front of their tortoises. And—"

"All of that good stuff, yes." I smiled at her. "You saved the pets from the aliens, Sergeant. You finally did it!"

"Payback is sweet." I couldn't see for sure through her helmet, but I heard the grudging smile in her voice. "I'm over the Moon!"

"Whereas frankly, I am SO over the Moon, already," Kimmy tutted. "Standing on another world is an interesting scientific experience, but I've had enough now and I want to go home."

"Home, yeah . . ." I turned to spy the Earth. There it hung in the darkness, billions of years old but still bursting with energy. So solid and strong – swinging the Moon around its middle every month, keeping its grip on the animals that swarmed over its surface in this quiet little backwater of space.

I want to go home too, I thought. And after all this, maybe I've got a real shot at making a new one. A *better* one.

"Remote on troll!" Little G declared, producing a little black box covered in dials and switches. "Hello! Hyper-beam, remote on troll!"

"Remote *control*," Ray corrected him.

"Hug!" Little G replied.

I stooped to pick up Herbert in his bowl, ready to make the journey back.

"No," my fish said firmly. "I am not going back with you."

"Huh?" I frowned down at him. "You're staying here?"

"I am going away," Herbert declared. "Someone

must journey into the outer reaches of the galaxy to find the Galactic Council . . . to make them understand that the Earth can *never* be sold. That it belongs now to the tiny beings that slowly – so slowly – grew up there. In their ignorance, they do not treat the planet at all well – but perhaps they can learn." He nodded sagely. "Yes, they will *have* to learn, in time. And they deserve a second chance."

"You're going off into space?" I said. "Alone?"

"Aside from my little glowing plastic jellyfish, quite so." Herbert nodded.

"But it's such a long, dangerous journey." I could feel wetness sting my eyes as I looked out of my spacesuit's goldfish bowl and into his. "You're a fish. Humans have treated your kind very badly. How come you're still willing to do this for them?"

Herbert wore a wistful smile. "I don't do it for all humankind, Tim . . . I do it for one kind human." He blinked. "I've watched you grow up. It would give me comfort, as I journey onward, to know that you will continue to grow in peace. And after all, once the antidote fills the Earth's air and water, goldfish will lose their gifts and return to normal." He smiled. "I prefer to go on learning . . . to find my destiny."

"You . . . You're one cool fish." I sniffed noisily, wishing I could wipe my eyes. "You know that, Herbert? A really cool fish."

"I am currently a few degrees below my ideal temperature, for sure, Tim." Herbert shivered. "What a good job my bowl can draw heat from the mini-retro jets built into the base. That'll keep me warm as aquatic toast." He waggled his fins and spun in a loop-the-loop as Elodie walked over. "Remember, you two. The new waters we swim in life may seem terribly chilly when first we enter. But they warm up. Yes, they soon grow warmer. So keep paddling, my friends . . . keep paddling . . ."

Then, the bowl shook, the water bubbled slightly, and with a swift, efficient SWOOSH, Herbert's little world took off into the vacuum, and streaked away into the distance. Before I could even call goodbye, he was gone.

"I hope he finds the Galactic Council OK," said Elodie. "If he gets lost, the Earth could still be sold on to any alien race who fancies it." She snorted softly. "Which means the fate of the human race depends on a goldfish!"

"Yeah," I said quietly. "But *what* a goldfish."

The TAMASSISS beside me waved a sudden arm. "Little G go home too. Bye-bye. Little G. Home. Byeeeee." He was already fading away.

"Little G, no!" I cried. "Don't just go!"

"You've got the hyper-beam remote control!" cried Ray.

"AND MY FLIPPIN' SUIT!" bawled Kimmy.

But she could shout all she liked – Little G had still gone. I gulped. He wouldn't really just abandon us up here, would he?

As if in answer, a red glow lit up our lonely mountain – and suddenly we were back in the base. Me, Elodie, Ray, Kimmy, Mum and Dad and Katzburger. All down and – unbelievably, against all the odds in the universe – safe.

Spontaneously, those of us still conscious burst into a wild, jumping dance of relief and victory.

But the TAMASSISS lay empty on its side. There

was no sign of Little G.

"I wonder where he went," said Elodie.

"Home, he said," I murmured. "Who knows where that is?" Then as I checked Dad was OK and held his hand, I remembered the Rubbish House had been burned to the ground. "Come to think of it, who knows where *my* home is?"

Katzburger gave me a scowling grin. "Don't you know, fool?"

"I do," said Kimmy.

"You're already there, Tim," said Ray. "Quite a place. And only about 107 billion, 802 million, 919 thousand, 700 previous not-very-careful owners."

"Ha! Of course." I threw open my arms and laughed. "The only home any of us have got! A kind-of-cool little planet we call . . . Earth."

FORTY

"When you nearly die, it's like you've been reborn," I said to Elodie, maybe the first or second day after Things Started Getting Back To Normal. "It's another chance at loving life. And you know what? I'm gonna live every last minute to the absolute fullest."

"Sure," drawled Elodie. "For the first week, anyway."

"No, I mean it!" I insisted.

"Well," she said, "guess you'll have to keep in touch, and let me know, eh?"

"Yeah." I shrugged, a bit embarrassed. "I guess I will."

Slowly, things got moving again.

Dad and Mum helped Ray and Kimmy with the anti-lullaby cure. First they brought round the base, then they helped the base to bring round the whole world. Weirdly, it seemed Dad and Mum found they actually quite liked working together, after all this time.

Sergeant Katzburger found she liked working more herself when she was immediately promoted to captain for her impeccable service in the defence of Earth.

Then the Big Suits decided they should buy the designs for the TAMASSISS and the antigravity pads from Kimmy. After weeks of some of the toughest negotiation ever witnessed, Kimmy made a cool fifty billion dollars from the deal. So rather than just go to Cambridge University next year, she's decided to buy it.

She's putting Ray in charge of the science department. Some of the old professors there kicked up a fuss, of course, but Kimmy sued their pants off. She and Ray should have an interesting time.

As for me . . . and Elodie . . . Well, that should be interesting too.

The military compensated my dad for destroying

our rubbish home. They've given him an incredible beach house/observatory/laboratory on a small island near Florida. It's entirely solar-powered and carbon-neutral. And of course, he can zip to work at the North Pole base by hyper-beam so there's no commute, while I can zip to my old school in the blink of an eye. The change in time zones is kind of tricky but I don't fall asleep in *too* many lessons.

It's kind of cool, being allowed to use an experimental instant travel system while Dad works to make it super-energy-efficient, so using it won't cost the Earth.

Sometimes I even hyper-beam round to grab a coffee with Helen.

And very occasionally I "accidentally" zip into Fist-Face's bedroom at midnight and run around his room pretending to be a ghost, or put custard in his football boots, or plastic dog turds in his lunchbox. You should see his face! No, actually, I wouldn't wish that on anyone.

Anyway, my mum is staying on at the North Pole too, doing more weirdo research. See, it's not just military stuff they do at the Pole now. They're developing all sorts of serious ways to start protecting the planet from the harm we cause it. Surprise, surprise, the GETs' repairs to the planet turned out to be a quick-fix con: Big Heal, Fat Nothing. Things were back to bad again in months.

Mum says, we'll just have to manage our muck for ourselves.

And even though she and Elodie still live in Ontario, we see quite a bit of them these days. They zipped over to check out our new place, and we had a pretty good dinner with NO organic cumbers of cu and NO tomatoes, and just . . . well, got on together.

Until suddenly, someone else turned up for dinner.

"HELLO!"

Little G, in a Hawaiian shirt, straw hat, shorts and an enormous medallion, glowed redly into being on top of the dining table – and then stepped in the trifle. "Oop! Oh dear. Dear G."

"Little G!" Elodie and I chorused.

Dad jumped up in surprise. "You're back!"

"What happened, Little G?" I asked him, helping

Mum to guide the funny little alien into a chair before he could tread in the lasagne too. "I thought you went home?"

"Uh-huh!" He reached out his long, sticky arms for me. "Little G ammmm home!"

Dad looked pale. "Er . . . Home? Here?"

"And home with Elodie!" Little G grabbed her too in a wonky hug. "Home, home, lots of homes for G! Got G wrong, see? See G?"

"Wrong?" I asked him. "What did you get wrong?"

"G in Little G not for Goldfish," he explained. "Hello! G for *Gooseheart*."

"Fantastic!" I said happily. "Dad, that's OK if Little G has a home with us, isn't it?"

"Isn't it, Mum?" Elodie added.

Mum laughed and hugged Little G too. "Well . . . why not!"

"As you say, why not." Dad's smile was strained, but it was there. "I suppose he's house-trained!"

"Thanks, Dad." I put an arm around him. He actually put his arm around me too. It was quite a moment. Then, **"HUGGGGGG!"** Little G threw his arms around us both, and knocked us both off our chairs and into the sideboard.

That was a while ago now. Me and Dad and Mum and Elodie – and Little G, of course – all get together a lot. But we do our own things too. We're all pretty different, and I guess we might take different routes through the years . . . You know. When we're ready.

But however old we get, and wherever we land up, I know that some kind of crazy gravity will always hold us together. Just as it holds Earth together with its solar system stablemates while we all whizz around through space.

Space is pretty big stuff. I've seen that for myself. But family?

Seems to me, that's a whole other universe.

Fin

A MYSTERIOUS PIG IN FANCY DRESS RUNS WILD!

If you noticed I spelled 'chapter' wrong at the top of the page, **CONGRATULATIONS!** I'm just making sure you're awake.

You may think it's a bit crazy to start a book with a wrongly-spelled word. Well, with the story I'm telling, you'd better get used to crazy. And I should warn you, we're talking **bonkers, fruit-loops, round-the-bend, round-the-twist, round-and-round-the-mulberry-bush-then-round-an-extra-twisty-bendy-fruit-loop crazy.** Not throwing the book away in disgust? Good. Then I'll continue. . .

The whole thing started when we saw a pig in a top hat running wild through the house. By "we", I mean my whole family: Mum, Dad and Lib.

Lib – or Liberty – is my little sister. My stupid, whiny, annoying little sister.

She was the first one to see the mysterious pig. . .
and to hear it, for that matter.

I was asleep at that point.

Who am I?

Glad you asked.

I'm Stew Penders, and this is my book.

Confession: it's my first go at writing a book and
I'm feeling my way a bit. So, please. . . bear with me.

There – a picture! I feel happier when there are
drawings involved, you see; I'm more of a comic
book kind of guy. I've been writing and illustrating my

own comics since **forever**.

Well, OK, I may have exaggerated slightly there. But from now on, I won't. I don't need to. This true-life story is crazy enough already.

I'll prove it. Let's get back to the night it all began. . .

There was Libs lying in her strange, unfamiliar bed – unfamiliar because we'd only moved into my granddad's old house that very day, and he'd left lots of old furniture behind, and Libs had whined and whined until Mum and Dad shut her up by saying she could have Granddad's big, wooden, sleigh-shaped bed in her room.

Anyway, there she was, surrounded by stuffed animals and princesses and all that rubbish, when suddenly. . .

Snuffle – snuffle —

There's a sinister snuffling outside her bedroom door. **"PIIIIIIG!!!"** Lib shrieked from across the landing, with way more exclamation marks than I can be bothered to write right now. **"PIIIIG!** In my BEDROOOOOOM!!! It's got a hat on! Big, fat, hairy **PIIIIIIIIIIIIIIIIIG!"**

Luckily for the accuracy of this eyewitness account, that was when I woke up. Nine times out of ten, my automatic response would be to shout something brotherly like, **"LIB, SHUT UP AND STOP BEING SO DUMB!"**

But, on this one-tenth of times, I didn't.

Partly that was because I was in a strange bedroom too, and got confused 'cos I didn't know where I was for a few seconds. But mainly it was because I heard a throaty squeal carry above Lib's cries. And, fair play to her, it did sound *exactly* like the sort of noise a big fat hairy **'PIIIIIG'** might make.

Nah, that's crazy, I told myself. Isn't it?

I checked my watch and saw it was after two in the morning. A split-second later I heard Dad throw open the door to his and Mum's room, which was next door to mine, and shamble outside.

"Something must've got in through the old cat-flap. . ." he said, sounding sleepy and confused. "I don't get it – I boarded the hole up with a piece of two-by-four, a good match for the door, it should've held, no problem. . ."

Dad is a bit of a Do-It-Yourself whizz – or so he likes to think. Eight times out of ten his DIY does it back to him.

But this was no ordinary night.

I was wide awake by now, and waiting for Dad to give Lib a roasting for being stupid, annoying, whiny etc and for making stuff up. But the next moment, *he* was shouting too!

"Bryony!" (That's my mum's name, sorry, should've mentioned that.) "Bryony, there really *is* a pig!"

I almost jumped out of my unfamiliar bed in shock. I heard more squeals and snuffling (by now it was hard to tell whether they were coming from Lib or the pig), quickly followed by a loud *thump* as Dad fell over.

"AAAGH!" he shouted. And then my mum joined in with the caterwauling. Or *pig*erwauling, I guess. Her conversation with Dad went like this:

Mum— "A pig?"

Dad— "Yes, a pig! It got past me, don't come out!"

"But, a PIG?"

"Yes! A pig. Must've got in through the—"

"You mean there's a **PIG IN THE HOUSE?**"